THE BAKER STREET

BOOK 3

MYSTERIES

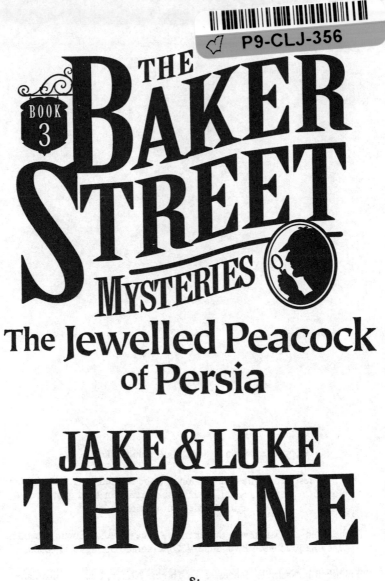

The Jewelled Peacock
of Persia

JAKE & LUKE
THOENE

Publishers Since 1798

THOMAS NELSON PUBLISHERS
Nashville

Published in association with the Literary Agency of Alive Communications,
1465 Kelly Johnson Blvd. Suite #320, Colorado Springs, CO 80920.

Published in Nashville, Tennessee, by Thomas Nelson, Inc., and distributed
in Canada by Word Communications, Ltd., Richmond, British Columbia,
and in the United Kingdom by Word (UK), Ltd., Milton Keynes England.

ISBN 0-7852-7080-9

Printed in the United States of America
1 2 3 4 5 6 7 — 04 03 02 01 00 99 98

For
Jacob Chance Thoene.
Welcome to our world.
You are loved.

PROLOGUE

PATRICK GANNON'S pale blue eyes studied the eroded rocky mound that brooded over the ruins of the ancient Persian city of Fars. Below the skull-shaped knob of sandstone stretched a desert valley. The ball of the setting sun hung low on the horizon like a giant, ripe orange ready to be picked. Many months of working in the dusty, wind-scoured conditions had baked Gannon's face to a leathery brown. A trickle of sweat dripped off his chin, disappearing quickly into the thirsty sand.

Gannon allowed his tired mind to wander. A blast of parching air howled past him, rustling his grizzled brown hair and beard. The dull clanking of a copper bell echoed from the lead ram of a wandering herd of sheep. The flock circled loosely, foraging in the desolation. They eliminated the few remaining scattered green specks from the clay-colored earth. The mark of their trail was a wide band that reached back to a distant horizon. Gannon followed the cleared swath with his eyes until the uniform brown of the desert floor merged with the tawny hills and the dust-colored sky.

Another gust of wind cannoned shards of gravel and dust painfully against Gannon's cheeks. He turned his head quickly to cover his eyes and squatted down with his back to the blow.

The change of position drew the archaeologist's attention to the men at work on the side of the hill just a few yards below him. In a long furrow dug between ancient mud walls, the sun glistened on the backs of the men in the excavation. With picks and spades, they shovelled out centuries of sand from a set of buried steps.

The pace of Gannon's thoughts increased. They were close! Soon he would know if the bribes paid to reveal a carefully guarded secret location would confirm only myth or fabulous reality. If the legend were true and the site correct, the stairs led down to a hidden inner chamber. And at the bottom of the stairs, sealed within a vault below the two-thousand-year-old walls of Fars, was the legendary Jewelled Peacock of Persia.

The Persian workers chanted as they dug. The tempo of the chorus quickened. The speedier rhythm meant "Dig faster! Dig faster!" Gannon had never before heard it shouted in such a lively tone.

The shovelers fought to keep up as the shiny spikes of the picks ripped out larger chunks with each blow. Suddenly a pick plunged through into empty space. A panel below the bottom step crumbled, and a rancid puff of stale air rushed around the workers' legs. It smelled of something dead and impossibly old.

A man clothed in a light linen robe hurried up from the diggings to the mound where Gannon stood. "Mista

Gah-non, Mista Gah-non," he called urgently in heavily accented English.

The scientist stood up to greet him. Gannon's eyes locked on the man's excited stare. "What have you found, Yadeen?"

Out of breath as he reached the top, Yadeen proclaimed, "Mista Gah-non, the men have broken through! The vault is open! Come, come!"

"Centuries of searchers," Gannon whispered thoughtfully, "and now it's mine."

Now Yadeen's excitement faded even as Gannon's increased. "But I must again warn you," Yadeen begged. "The crown has been protected! It has remained undisturbed for twelve centuries, watched over by the Guardian. The Guardian will not be happy if you take the crown away from Persia. The curse says . . ."

Yadeen was cut off abruptly by Gannon. "I know! The curse falls on whoever removes the Peacock Crown from its hiding place." The archaeologist sounded irritated, and he stepped away from the foreman of the dig.

"But that is not all!" Yadeen grabbed the Englishman's arm firmly, stopping him. He continued in a low, trembling voice. "The curse says that the spirit guardian of the crown will search in the night for the one who has stolen it. And when the Guardian finds the thief who removed the Peacock Crown from its nest, then will come the fanning of the peacock's tail." Yadeen paused to raise his arms slowly up from his sides until they formed an arch above his head. "At such a time," he whispered urgently, "snakes will hatch from the earth to slay him for his greed."

Even while shaking his head in disbelief, Gannon leaned closer, intent on what Yadeen was saying.

"And that is not the worst of it, Mista Gah-non, for the snakes will not kill quickly! They will only inject their venom so that the thief cannot run away." Yadeen's eyes opened wide, and he pressed his fingers to his temples. "They will burrow into his eye sockets while he still lives, lay their eggs, and devour his brain!"

Patrick Gannon stood frozen for a moment at the mental image of what could happen to him if the curse were true. Then he shook his head. "No, no," he insisted, forcefully. "I'm not going to fall for that, Yadeen. I'm an archaeologist, not an astrologer. I don't believe in crystals or curses or spirits that hatch murderous snakes."

"But the curse!" Yadeen argued, frantic now. "I fear for your life!"

Gannon shook his head. "I've worked too hard for any curse, cult, or spirit to get in the way." He shrugged loose Yadeen's hand from his shoulder and strode toward the excavation pit.

A shout erupted from the men in the shaft. Gannon walked briskly, then broke into a trot. At his command the swarm of diggers formed a relay line. From hand to hand they transported a shining golden object out of the excavation and up the hill, the way a London fire brigade would pass buckets of water to put out a burning house.

The archaeologist met the find halfway up. With reverence he put out his hands to receive the jewel-studded, solid gold crown. Even in the hot desert air the object felt cold to the touch and was heavier than its size indicated. It had a hammered finish as smooth as melting ice. On the front of the ring of precious metal was a finely worked peacock figure about four inches tall. To the sides of the miniature bird were tail feathers formed of braided gold. They had large green and red stones on the tips and when unfolded would curve over the head. Despite the heat, a chill ran down Gannon's back as the fiery ruby eyes in the peacock's head seemed to follow him when he moved the crown in the light.

Moments earlier, Gannon thought, the Jewelled Peacock of Persia was only a myth, a legend, the stuff of dreams and fables; now it was a priceless treasure, finally recovered and in his possession! It would make him and his sponsor very rich men. It was an occasion to celebrate! Gannon quickly forgot Yadeen's warning. Later, when he remembered the curse at all, he dismissed it quickly, but not without shuddering.

—————

The triangular goat-hide door to the tent flapped violently in the howling desert wind. A sandstorm drew close to the lonely camp, the grains hitting the roof and walls like tiny bullets.

Gathered in a circle on the floor in the dim interior were six men. All members of a band called the Guardians of the Peacock, these fierce warriors were descended from the Assassins of the Middle Ages. The original form of their name, *hashashin*, referred to the drug hashish, which they took before their bloodthirsty attacks.

The men talked seriously, sharing a pipe. An old, white-bearded man sat at the head of the discussion. He listened patiently while the younger men argued.

". . . I think we must take it back now, before they leave the territory," one man stated.

"No, that is not right," a slightly older man argued. "They already have the crown. Let the curse do its work. What need has it of our assistance?"

The pipe was passed to another warrior who joined the argument. "The honor of our society and the pride of our cause is at stake. We should strike now!"

"Now they are ready for us," a fourth guardian declared. "They have just retrieved the crown and are expecting an attack soon. We should wait until they are miles from Fars and then attack at night when they believe themselves safe from harm."

This comment aroused approval from the elder. He pushed the pipe to his lips, deeply breathing in the green smoke. All waited for him to speak. "The young one is right. Here they are ready. I will not risk a challenge from the British army. And there is that perfidious dog, the Shah of Qajar." The old man spat noisily before continuing. "If we are to take back the crown so that I, Giyan Hissar, may sit on the throne, then you must strike in the night as a small group of bandits. Only then will we escape failure and death without reward. Elam Zagros?" he said, passing the pipe across to the only man who had not spoken.

"Yes, Hissar, I think that is the wisest way," a figure with jet black hair and a scraggly moustache agreed. The whites of Zagros's eyes burned a fierce yellow, fueled by his passion for the crown and the kingdom. "Tonight we ride into battle!" he shouted, rallying the men. "And we will recapture the crown and reclaim the throne for Persia!"

The tent erupted with screaming warriors. They ran outside, shooting their guns into the air and brandishing their wickedly curved swords before readying their horses for battle.

———

Just out of earshot of the uproar in the Guardians' camp, Patrick Gannon mounted his camel for the long journey across the desert to the sea. With him he carried the Peacock Crown, enough food and water for a week's travel, and his Martini single-shot rifle. The rest of the expedition, fifteen more armed men on camels, pulled in line to follow him.

After riding all evening and all night, they made camp at daybreak, having covered seventy miles. Gannon dozed off, but nightmares of the curse woke him. Then his fear of attacks from Persian patriots kept him awake.

He had just begun to nod off again when he was startled by the arrival of a band of nomads. Peering through an opening in the tent, Gannon clutched his loaded rifle tightly with both hands while the newcomers dismounted outside.

Yadeen stood up to greet them as they neared the encampment. Gannon decided to stay inside and keep the crown guarded.

A tense moment followed while Gannon waited to see what the nomads would do. The one who seemed to be in charge conversed with some of Gannon's men. Smiling, the leader hunkered down to talk. One of the hired porters brought him a cup of coffee. He nodded in a friendly way while he and Yadeen talked.

It was all too relaxed. Suspecting the worst, Gannon scurried to the back of the tent. Lifting up the edge of the tarp, he looked for signs that this visit was a decoy, while the real attack came from behind. There was nothing in sight but a scarp of rock and thin brush.

Spending the next half hour hurrying back and forth between the front and the back of the tent, Gannon kept a constant watch for danger. But no attack came. The nomad finished his coffee, thanked Yadeen, and returned to his mount.

After the wandering tribesmen had left, Gannon exited his tent. "What did he say, Yadeen?" he inquired.

Yadeen shrugged. "He wanted coffee, and he asked what we are doing out here with no goats and no sheep."

"What did you tell him?"

"I tell him we on our way to the sea, to a big ship soon."

"No!" Gannon shouted angrily. "You didn't tell him that, did you, Yadeen?"

"Oh yes," Yadeen answered, dismissing the worry with a wave of his hand. "He's friendly. No need to worry, Mis-tah Gah-non."

"How do you know it's not a trap?"

"That is a clan leader from the mountains. They are peaceful herders."

"And you never know, do you?" Gannon scolded. "Tell the men to pack; we leave in half an hour."

The expedition travelled without rest through the hottest part of the day. The sun beat down unbearably, like a roaring furnace in the midst of a burning building. Gannon added ninety miles of circuitous travel to the trek, hoping to avoid trouble.

At last they reached the Persian Gulf. Gannon calculated that they were fifty miles north of the small harbor where they were to find the freighter and safety. He finally allowed his men to stop. They would again try to rest by day and travel when darkness hid their movements.

When it came, the Persian night was one of the blackest Gannon had ever seen, even after the moon rose. The thin silver crescent cast very little light over the naked sand along the gulf.

The last leg of the journey found the company between a steep mountain range on the left and the waters of the gulf on the right. The trail turned abruptly. It entered rocky terrain and led down into a narrow canyon. Sheer rock walls more than one hundred feet high bordered each side of the path.

Five miles into the canyon, the advance scout came galloping back to the caravan as if something were wrong. Gannon lifted his right hand, signalling the men behind him to stop. As the scout approached, Gannon noticed something odd and said to his second in command, "Do you notice anything different about the scout, Yadeen?"

Yadeen examined the figure as he drew closer. "Yes, he . . . he looks almost bigger, or something . . ."

Waiting not another second, Gannon swung the rifle upward without waiting to put it to his shoulder. The counterfeit scout also fired his weapon, but Gannon was a touch faster. The attacker somersaulted off his camel, which continued to gallop forward.

Yells and curses came from all sides of the canyon, followed by gunfire. Gannon dove six feet to the ground from the back of his mount. Hitting the earth hard, the archaeologist crawled to a pile of rocks for cover.

Inexperienced with firearms, many of Gannon's men were shot down before they even had a chance to fire.

Frightened camels scurried in all directions. Yadeen's animal was hit. It fell on Yadeen's leg, pinning him to the ground. The others who survived the fierce assault ran for the rocks.

Yadeen lay out in the open. He wiggled his rifle out from under his camel's belly and cocked it. Taking aim at a whooping bandit, he fired. But the weight of the animal had bent the barrel of his weapon, and when he fired the gun blew up in Yadeen's face. He fell back with a groan.

Gannon saw his dreams of the crown fleeing and his own life about to be sacrificed as well. But the archaeologist was not a man to give up easily. He held his fire until the attackers drew closer.

Leaving the concealment of their ambush, the raiders charged the ragged remains of the caravan from front and rear. Gannon's remaining men fired, and three of the enemy were shot out of their saddles. But the exchange of gunfire was not even. One by one, the weapons in the caravan fell still, until Gannon alone was left. He waited silently.

There were fewer of the bandits left than he had thought. Only three men climbed down to loot the saddlebags. Gannon's pulse raced as one of the attackers approached his position. Suddenly, out of the corner of his eye, the archaeologist saw Yadeen lift a pistol. Yadeen's right hand hung limp, and he cocked the hammer with his bloody chin.

At the sound, one of the raiders turned. Yadeen pulled the trigger. The man fell to the ground, but before Yadeen could ready the gun again, he was killed.

Gannon saw the last two bandits look nervously around. Gannon quickly fired his first shot, knocking one of the men flat. The other spun and dropped into a crouch, trying to tell where the bullet had come from.

Quickly loading another cartridge into the rifle, Gannon took careful aim. Hearing the noise of the breach lever, the last bandit spotted Gannon.

Moving as if in slow motion, both men raised their guns at the same time. Gannon's eyes were wide and his jaw dropped. His sights swung over the man's throat, and he fired. A crash that seemed louder than any before left a gray cloud of smoke between them. The attacker's gun fell to the ground and blasted a last round into the body of a dead camel.

Gannon picked himself up, trembling with fear. Were there more men out there who wanted the crown—and would kill to get it? There was no time to bury the bodies. Every minute could mean the approach of another bandit horde.

Muttering a short prayer, Gannon caught a lone stray camel. He grabbed his pack and galloped for the harbor.

Even though he reached the harbor safely, Patrick Gannon did not relax until the rusty steamer was at sea. It was another whole day and night before he allowed himself to sleep.

ONE

THE STEPS LEADING to the tall white columns at the front of St. Martin-in-the-Fields Church seemed to dance in the heat that rose from the cobblestones. Mist from the fountains across the street in Trafalgar Square settled quietly back into the pools on the windless afternoon. All sounds thundered into the still air. The hoofbeats of every cart horse echoed like an entire cavalry regiment. People moved slowly about their business in the heart of Queen Victoria's London. Ladies in ankle-length dresses wilted under their parasols. Gentlemen suffering in tailored wool suits and high, stiff-collared shirts sweated and squinted at the bright day.

Carriages and two-wheeled hansom cabs stopped in front of the church to let out a steady stream of people wearing solemn expressions on their perspiring faces. They hurried gratefully into the cool shade of the portico. From beneath the Royal Coat of Arms carved over the entrance, the late arrivals heard the organ trumpet out a brief introduction to a hymn. Then young voices began to sing:

The Son of God goes forth to war;
A kingly crown to gain.
His bloodred banner streams afar.
Who follows in its train?

The melody bounced off the high ceiling, filling the simple box of the sanctuary with a sweet harmony that soothed the mourning listeners. Nearly every seat on the hard wooden benches was filled as the upper class of London society came to pay their last respects to George Beardsley, Lord Scimonoce.

Towering head and shoulders above his fellows, Duff Bernard looked comical in the undersized choir gown that only reached down to mid-thigh. The legs of his patched and mended pants were visible below. He did sing beautifully, however, much to the constant surprise of Choir Director Ingram, who was also the headmaster of the Waterloo Road Ragged School where Duff slept and got his meals.

At Duff's side, his friend Danny Wiggins smiled as Duff projected his voice perfectly in tune with the rest of the choir. As the song came to a close and the chorus was seated, red-haired Peachy Carnehan leaned toward Danny and whispered, "Amazing, ain't it? Half the time you can't understand what Duffer's talking about, but he sings like an angel."

Danny, catching a stern look from Headmaster Ingram, just glared at Peachy, then turned to Duff and patted him on the back. Duff smiled.

The memorial service lasted almost two hours, and the sanctuary grew warmer and warmer. While most of the boys in the choir were nodding off, Danny noticed that Duff looked relaxed and contented as he stared up the length of the church toward the large crucifix.

Peachy was fully asleep and slumping on Danny's shoulder. Peachy gave a tremendous jerk in his seat when the organ began playing "A Mighty Fortress Is Our God," signaling that the service was over. After the mourners had filed out, Ingram excused the choir, and Danny, Duff, and Peachy went to speak with him.

"Well, boys," the tall, muscular man teased in a soft, reverent tone. "Did you have nice naps?"

Danny blushed and lowered his head.

"To be fair, sir," Peachy said, "I don't think Duffer slept a wink."

Duff grinned again and looked triumphantly at the headmaster.

"Peachy," Danny said with mock astonishment, "that's the first time you've ever talked good about Duff."

Carnehan looked stunned by the thought. "I was just about to say he should be plenty rested . . . what with all the daydreamin' he does."

Older by three years than his friends but slower in thought, Duff put up with a lot of good-natured teasing from Peachy. Together, Danny, Duff, and Peachy were the Baker Street Brigade, partners in detective work with the great Sherlock Holmes.

On such a miserably sweaty summer day, the only mystery in Peachy's mind was how he would ever get cool again. A quick splash in a fountain, perhaps, before the constables ran them off?

It was nearly five o'clock, and the air outside the church was still like an oven. Darting down the steps, the boys nearly ran over the silver-haired earl of Shaftesbury, founder of the Waterloo Road Ragged School and many other homes for orphans like it. "Ah, Wiggins, Carnehan, and Bernard. So good to see you. Duff, I must commend you on your singing. It was marvelous. All of you did well. Please thank the other choir boys for assisting in the service."

Duff hung his head in shy embarrassment and peered up at the earl through shaggy locks of dark hair.

"We're sorry about your friend," Danny said, "but you did give 'im a right nice farewell."

"It was splendid," said the earl. "Of course, I knew Lord Scimonoce for many years in the R.G.S. He was a fine man."

"Argiss?" Peachy repeated, looking confused.

"No, lad. R. G. S. The Royal Geographical Society. Lord Scimonoce and I served together on many committees with other R.G.S. fellows."

"What do they do?" Danny asked.

"The R.G.S. is Her Majesty's commissioned fellowship of exploration. We sponsor exciting expeditions, excavations in strange foreign lands, voyages of discovery—that sort of thing. Those of us too old to accompany such explorations merely fund them, but we all look forward to the results with great anticipation. George Beardsley, as honorary corresponding secretary for antiquities, had a particular interest in ancient Persian ruins. His life's

dream was just fulfilled by one of our sponsored archae-
ologists—the discovery of a fabulous crown called the
Jewelled Peacock of Persia—but Beardsley didn't live to
see it."

"Cor!" Peachy said. "That's tough!"

"Quite right, Carnehan," the earl agreed. Then,
shaking his head angrily as if dismissing an unpleasant
thought, he continued, "But don't believe that rubbish
about the curse."

Peachy's eyes went wide. "What curse?" he asked.
All thoughts of diving into the pools in Trafalgar Square
were forgotten. "A buried treasure *and* a curse?"

Just then a stylish black carriage with a coat of arms
emblazoned on the door rolled to a stop at the curb.

Duff spoke up, pointing at the coach and uniformed
attendants. "Is that yours?" he asked the earl.

Lord Shaftesbury turned and smiled. "Quite right,
Duff. I must be off, gentlemen." Peachy glared at Duff
for distracting the earl. "If you care to see the crown, it
is arriving this evening at the British Museum for exhibition there. Good day to you." The earl waved from
the window, and the carriage clattered away down the
road.

The British Museum was a long, hot walk from the
church, and the trip would take the boys twice as far from
their home at the school as they were now. But Danny
and Peachy needed no discussion about what their evening's activity would be. With quick nods and an exchange of smiles they each grabbed one of Duff's elbows
and set off for the greatest collection of ancient artifacts
in the world—the British Museum.

No matter if the day is sunny, it always seems to go gray after a funeral. Peachy, Danny, and Duff walked thoughtfully down St. Martin's Lane. The whole business of Lord Beardsley's death reminded Peachy of how his parents had been killed in Africa. He remembered something that an orphan named Adam had told him just after Peachy first came to stay at Waterloo Road Ragged School: "You know, Peachy, whenever I get to feelin' down, I just chin up. 'Cause guys like you and me, we ain't got much but our friends and a mind to choose. And when that's where you're at, life's as good as your attitude." Peachy understood what Adam meant about being positive and making the most of every day, no matter how lousy it was.

"So whatever happened to Adam Everett anyhow?" Peachy asked, surprising Danny with a name he had not heard in a long time.

"I don't know." Danny's eyes lit up with remembrance. "What brought him to mind?"

"Ah, I was just recalling what a good chap he was," Peachy remarked.

"Moved to America or something, with an rich uncle or . . ." Danny tried to recall.

Duff trudged along beside. "Him was nice," the large boy agreed. "Danny, think we'll ever see him again?"

Danny smiled. "You never can tell, Duff. Sometimes you make friends that'll last a lifetime." The boy sobered again as he thought about Lord Scimonoce's funeral. "And sometimes, before you realize it, they go away just like that," he concluded, snapping his fingers.

Peachy pondered Danny's comment. He took his friends for granted, expecting them to always be around. Yet each one had important qualities that he would miss dreadfully if anything happened to any of them.

Take the Baker Street Brigade, for example. Danny had a mind for solving cases. Without him, they would never get into the mysterious adventures that they did. And Duff was the protector; even though Peachy and Danny frequently had to look out for him, Duff always came through when they needed him the most. Besides, Duff's simple mind always had a way of making them laugh. It made Peachy happy to have such good friends. Brothers they were and would be until the day they died.

Peachy wondered what his own role was. He was unsure of who he would be when they all grew up. But for the time being they were young and excited. On a confident note he added, "You never know, Duff. Sometimes those same friends will turn up again when you least expect it."

Duff gave Peachy a broad smile and bounced his head yes as they walked along. Duff wiped the sweat off his head with his arm. "I'm thirsty. Can we get some fruit ice?"

"There you go, wanting to spend all your hard-earned money on food again," Danny chuckled.

"But it's hot," Duff complained. "And I keep seeing that big red strawberry ice. I taste it in my head."

Even though he chuckled at Duff's expression, Peachy's mouth began to water. "That does sound good. Come on, Danny. What do you say, mate?"

"Why not?" Danny agreed. "There's always a fruit ice man on the corner of New Oxford and Charing Cross

Road. And then afterward, we can go on to the museum."

"Right-o!" Peachy could tell the day was getting better already.

They each bought a strawberry ice for a penny and ate it while dangling their arms over the bars of the museum fence. Duff ate his the fastest, as usual, licking the drips that ran down the paper cone until his chin had a pink streak.

"Look there, Peachy," Danny said, pointing through the bars. "Crushers by that carriage."

"Too right!" Peachy noted. "Must be something valuable in there." Looking around, Peachy searched for suspicious characters. Great Russell Street and the other roads near the British Museum were pretty empty. But he spotted one man in an alley across the street. The figure was wearing a black, hooded cloak that covered his face. The garb seemed too hot for such a blistering day, but then London was full of unusual characters in dress more strange than that. The man appeared to be watching the carriage too. "Maybe that's a load of the Persian stuff," Peachy said, changing his focus back to the guards and the carriage.

"Could be," Danny agreed. "Like that mysterious golden crown."

A green-coated porter descended from the wide steps, which spanned the entire front of the British Museum. He lifted a crate out of the carriage and pivoted to face the enormous Grecian-style building.

"It's gonna be five o'clock before you know it," Duff whined. "And I don't want to miss dinner."

"You ready to go home, Peachy?" Danny asked.

"I guess so." Peachy curiously glanced back to see what the man in the alley was doing. But the hooded man was gone. Peachy ducked his head against the glare off the windows of the Museum Tavern, but the figure had truly disappeared. Then Peachy's attention was pulled away as another man, lean and athletic, jumped down from the carriage and ran up the museum steps behind the porter. The boys pulled their arms out of the fence and turned to head home. Peachy took one last look. Trotting between the three-story pillars that fronted the museum, the thin man from the carriage disappeared through the massive entrance door.

Patrick Gannon's boots echoed loudly off the steps and reverberated under the colonnade of the British Museum. The archaeologist passed through the entry onto the gray marble floor of the vestibule. He was so intent on the business at hand that he did not even spare a glance for the Roman Gallery that opened on his left. Two stern-faced guards flanking the green-uniformed porter followed Gannon as the foursome marched straight ahead into the gigantic hall of the copper-domed Reading Room. The porter struggled with a small but awkwardly shaped wooden crate.

Completed in 1857 as a new addition to the museum, the Reading Room was one of the largest in the world. Intellectual home to many distinguished writers and scholars, the Reading Room was an invaluable resource that contained more than 200,000 books and manuscripts. But despite the fact that the library was visited by a thousand researchers a day, it was still the least famous part of the museum.

Gannon strode purposefully, as if he did not even see the crowd of scholars who peered over the tops of their books to watch the little procession. Exiting at the rear of the hall, he followed a red carpet up several stairs and into the North Gallery. He turned right at the Fourth Egyptian Room with its scarab jewelry dating from 4000 B.C. and entered the Assyrian and Babylonian Room. The scientist hesitated in front of a pair of dark oak doors. Then, as if making up his mind suddenly, he gave three sharp raps on the panel.

"Come in," a hearty, booming voice invited. Gannon was immediately face-to-face with Douglas Macintire, the American promoter and showman. Macintire stood up behind a wide, clean desk. His broad, jowly face split into a wide smile. He extended his fleshy hand. "Ha! Patrick, you're back at last! A triumph! A monumental achievement!" Two other men stood behind Macintire, but they observed the greeting without speaking.

Gannon shook Macintire's hand firmly but with less enthusiasm than the American. "Quite good to be back." He sighed deeply.

Macintire's attention shifted abruptly from Gannon to the wooden crate in the porter's arms. "Is that it?" he questioned, motioning to the box. His words vibrated with ill-concealed excitement.

Gannon nodded. "Set it down here," he instructed the porter. "Carefully!" he admonished needlessly.

The short man transporting the container flushed with pride at the importance of his job. He gently placed the small crate on the desk. A halo of fine dust from three thousand miles of travel clouded the air.

"Was it rough getting out?" Macintire asked, tearing his concentration away from the box.

Gannon turned his pale eyes to study the American's face, as if to say, *Need you ask?* "I was forced to travel a hundred miles out of the way, while dodging Persian nationalists, nomads, and bandit chiefs. Every chap across two continents wanted something . . . coffee, money, or the crown, although I dare say they would all have been hot after the crown had they known what was in my saddlebag. Utter chaos, except for the cooperation of the Shah of Qajar."

Macintire nodded his understanding. "He's just a puppet ruler installed by Her Majesty's government," Macintire responded, "but useful anyway. Any casualties?"

Gannon's gaze fell to the floor, and his forehead creased in pain. "A few," he said. "There was . . ."

"Thanks, men," Macintire interrupted shortly, waving a dismissal to the hovering escort. "We'll take it from here."

The porter bobbed his head respectfully and exited the room quickly, with the guards close behind.

Quickly changing the subject, Macintire said, "You've met Lawrence Dreyer?"

Gannon had not paid any attention to the two men standing near the bright glare of the windows. The archaeologist blinked, squinting his bushy eyebrows to see a figure of medium build and pale complexion advancing on Macintire's left. The man introduced as Dreyer had short, grayish hair that receded slightly and a pallor of skin that argued against his ever having gone out in daylight. Gannon leaned forward to shake hands. Dreyer's was cool and limp. "No, I don't think I have had the pleasure."

"So good to finally meet you, Professor Gannon." Dreyer smiled. "I've heard a great deal about your explorations."

Macintire continued the introduction. "Mr. Dreyer is the new curator of Persian antiquities here at the museum. And this is Inspector Lestrade of Scotland Yard, here to consult on the matter of security."

"How do you do, sir?" Gannon greeted the short, pudgy policeman.

Lestrade took off his round bowler hat. "Pleasure," he replied in a condescending way. "So you had a bit of a scrape then? Killed a few desert beggars?" His tone suggested that he could not understand why moving a bit of old jewelry would present any problems at all.

Shocked at Lestrade's nonchalant manner, Gannon could not think of a reply and only looked at the detective. Lestrade breathed loudly through his nose, making a little whistling sound with each breath. His hair was parted down the middle, and he looked as arrogant as a cat. Gannon instantly disliked the man.

Sensing the tension, Macintire again changed the subject. "Well, what are we waiting for? Let's see it. It must be even more beautiful than I imagined." The American handed Gannon a small pry bar and inclined his head toward the crate.

Taking up the tool, Gannon began breaking loose the lid. He was grateful for the activity.

"So what are you afraid of now, Professor Gannon?"

Lestrade prodded. "You don't think a band of tribesmen will ride up Great Russell Street on their camels, do you? Can't think no chieftain, or vagabond, or any other sort of sheet-wearing hooligan would risk doing a stretch in Newgate Prison for a bit of old trinket."

The nails squawked in the soft, dry wood. The sound of protest was a perfect mirror of Gannon's thoughts about the inspector. "My concerns are . . ." He pried up the last corner and laid the lid on the desk blotter. ". . . a small band of Persian nationalists known as the Guardians of the Peacock. They're completely dedicated to reinstating the ancient Persian kingdom and removing the Shah of Qajar and anything British. The crown is sacred to them, and they'll do anything to get it back."

"Are they violent?" Macintire interjected.

"Very," Gannon affirmed. "One would be correct to say fanatical. They believe in the mystical importance of the crown and the curse that accompanies it." Gannon pulled a handful of sawdust out of the crate.

"A curse!" Curator Dreyer responded. "How thrilling! What does it say?"

"Pish-tosh," Lestrade snapped. "Do you gentlemen really need my expertise for this? Curses and hobgoblins?"

Even Macintire seemed fed up with the detective's attitude now. "Inspector, are you implying that we are wasting your time?"

Lestrade was preparing another mocking reply when all conversation ceased. The first sight of the circlet of gold seemed to steal the words from their lips when Gannon lifted it from the box. Even Lestrade was silent as the

Jewelled Peacock Crown gleamed magnificently in the golden afternoon light.

The archaeologist explained the history of the crown while the others remained in awed silence. "The crown was made for Ardashir I, king of the Persians in A.D. 224. We have proof of the date, as the king commissioned statues of himself wearing it."

Macintire picked up the crown, closely examining every stone, every facet. He held it up in the air in both hands, almost as if he would set it on his own head, but respectfully did not.

Continuing the tale, Gannon added, "It was passed down from ruler to ruler for four hundred years, until Persia was conquered by Moslem Arabs. The defeated Persians hid the crown in an underground vault to keep the Moslems from destroying it as they did all other graven images. In other digs we have found the lopped-off heads of statues, including Ardashir's."

The American promoter returned the crown to its sawdust nest without offering to let either Dreyer or Lestrade hold it. "Any other pieces?"

Gannon shrugged. "Nothing but a few brass artifacts and some coins. We made such haste to get out with the crown that I did not stop to carry anything else." He stopped to give Lestrade a pointed look. "I hear it was all looted the day after we departed."

The policeman snapped his fingers at the admission, as if Gannon were somehow at fault. Grudgingly, Lestrade inquired, "So do these nationalists have names? Who are their leaders?"

"I can remember a couple." Patrick Gannon thought for a minute. "Giyan Hissar is an elder, a tribal wise man in Persia. He wants to retrieve the throne from the Qajar Dynasty, but he needs the crown to prove his claim." Gannon's eyes scanned the ceiling as if looking for answers written there. "The only other I can think of is an assassin named Elam Zagros. I've heard he is the cult leader of the Guardians of the Peacock. I believe it was his group that attacked my caravan."

"What's his game then?" Inspector Lestrade asked.

The archaeologist frowned, uncertain about Lestrade's sudden apparent interest. "As I said earlier, he also wants to steal back the crown. With it, thousands more Persians would join his faction. The uprising would install Hissar on the throne and eliminate all foreign influence." Gannon looked around the group. "If we have any trouble, I'm certain it'll be from his group."

"Well then," Lestrade puffed with importance. "Now you've come to the point. No mumbo jumbo. It sounds like I've got my work cut out for me too. So I'll be off. We'll watch every seaport . . . no desert bandits will get past me."

"See what you can do, Inspector," Macintire said dryly. "Thanks."

"I'll show him out," Curator Dreyer announced, and he and the policeman left the room.

Gannon sighed with relief. "That man is seven kinds of a fool. Undoubtedly the Guardians are already here." Then shaking off the worrying thoughts he asked, "So we're on for tomorrow night?"

Macintire answered, "Right, tomorrow night. By the way, did you hear about George Beardsley's death?"

"Only just." Gannon shook his head. "It's a shame that someone who worked as hard on this project as he did won't get to see the crown's arrival. All the same, he did a good job getting the location of the recovery site. I could have been digging for ten more years without success if Beardsely had not uncovered the secret." Then in an overly casual tone Gannon asked, "Was there anything . . . unusual . . . about his death?" The archaeologist rubbed his beard and then his eyes. He was suddenly very tired.

Macintire took a deep breath before answering. "Heart attack. Never heard George had any heart trouble, but there you go. Happens all the time to people who seem to be fit as fiddles." He shrugged. "So. Tomorrow night, you'll be here?"

"Tomorrow it is," Gannon agreed and without further conversation they shook hands and parted.

TWO

LIGHTHEARTED LAUGHTER and the bright clinking of shiny silver filled the Assyrian Salon of the British Museum. Displaying around its walls stone carvings from Ninevah, the glass-roofed hall was, for the evening, the scene of a banquet. A hundred or so hungry guests sat around thirteen oak dining tables. At the far end of the room, slightly raised above the rest, the head table stretched the width of the room. It was placed just below a dramatic carving of King Assurbanipal hunting lions six hundred years before Christ.

Seated at the head table were the thirteen chief officers of the Royal Persian Antiquities Society and the evening's honored visitors. Among the guests were the earl of Shaftesbury, Patrick Gannon, and Douglas Macintire. The American promoter sat in the center of the platform because he was to be the key speaker for the night's event.

At the back of the room, watching and commenting on the posh display, was the Baker Street Brigade. On this occasion they were neither in their street clothes nor wearing their choir robes, but were dressed in long white serving uniforms.

Peachy stared at the multiple sets of silver serving trays. He knew that their price would feed the orphans of Waterloo Road Ragged School for a year. Danny saw the calculations going through Peachy's mind, then turned to watch Duff lick his lips at the sight of a huge platter of Dover sole. "Come on," he urged them both, "time for us to collect the next course." *Before Duff knaps the food and Peachy snaffles the silver,* he thought.

The three friends hurried along the Nimrod and Ninevah Galleries until they arrived at the kitchen temporarily set up in the western corner of the building. They surrendered their empty trays and received full ones to transport back to the serving staff in the banquet room.

"Look sharp, mates," Danny urged as he steadied the hot plates of food. "Duff, don't be licking your fingers."

The big boy ducked his head at the rebuke, then smiled when he saw that Danny was teasing.

The soup course had been followed by the fish course, and the fish course gave way to the roast. But it was not until after the dessert had been served that the Baker Street Brigade finally had time to catch their breath.

"Blimey, what a chore!" Peachy said. "Right! Now we can relax until after the speeches." He sounded relieved.

Duff would rather have hung around the kitchen hoping for a sample, but at Danny's urging he and Peachy returned to the banquet hall to watch the proceedings.

Douglas Macintire stood up and gently tapped a spoon on his crystal water glass to call the audience to attention. Just in front of him on the table sat a cloth-covered object. "Ladies and gentlemen of the Royal Persian Antiquities Society, I would like to welcome you all to this special reception. This occasion marks a signal triumph in the history of the R.P.A.S. With the help of your generosity and support, the society has been able to collect sixteen new valuable pieces, including the highlight and centerpiece of the collection, the Jewelled Peacock of Persia."

Like a conjurer revealing a rabbit in his hat, Macintire pulled off the white covering to reveal the Peacock Crown, protected in a glass case.

The crowd was quick to set down their coffee cups and napkins to applaud him.

Macintire continued, "This rare and priceless artifact lay undisturbed and undiscovered in the lost city of Fars for twelve hundred years. May it remain at least another dozen centuries secure in the arms of the British Museum."

The audience applauded again, and cries of "Hear, hear!" rang throughout the hall. But before Macintire had time to continue, the newly installed electric lights flickered wildly, then winked out, plunging the room into darkness. The guests were startled into silence, then they erupted into nervous chatter and demands for someone to do something.

Duff fumbled around, trying to keep his balance in the dark. "Cor, Danny! What's goin' on?"

"Relax, Duff. The lights will get put right in a tick or two."

Macintire attempted to settle the crowd. Tapping louder on his glass, he called, "Ladies and gentlemen, please stay calm. There's nothing to be alarmed about. I'm sure it's just a flaw in the new electric lighting system. We'll have it on again shortly."

"Crikey! Do you think it's that Jewelled Peacock's evil curse?" Peachy wondered aloud.

Danny snorted. "Don't be a ninny! That sort of thing isn't real."

Waiters carried oil lamps to all the tables. Soon the room was filled with light from dim yellow flames trailing streamers of black smoke up to the dark ceiling. In the flickering light, the lions in the hunting scenes on the walls appeared to move.

A tall waiter with broad shoulders approached the boys from behind. "Two of you come with me," he ordered.

"Where are we going, sir?" Peachy asked.

"It's this blinking electricity thing," the waiter explained. "Somewhere in the basement there's a fuse blown or some such thing. You," he pointed at Peachy, "and you," he indicated Danny, "are going to help me find it." He pushed them ahead of him toward the stairs.

Danny turned back to Duff and said, "It's all right, Duff. We won't be gone long." Duff looked nervous, but he nodded. Danny gave him the thumbs-up sign and turned to catch up with Peachy and the waiter.

———

With a dozen lanterns in place, the room brightened and the audience quieted. But the Assyrian Salon still felt really scary to Duff, though he did not know why. Maybe it was the way the eyes of the statues seemed to watch him, then look away when he noticed. Or maybe it was the burgundy-curtained alcoves between the groups of carvings that someone could be hiding behind.

Duff shivered at the thought, then quickly spun around to see if anyone was watching him. He caught sight of the glass-encased crown, gleaming dully in the lamplight. Maybe it was not the room at all . . . this evil feeling . . . maybe it was actually the Jewelled Peacock, glowing iridescently, that was the most frightening thing.

Even though the glare of the lamps on the glass case made it difficult to see the crown, it seemed to be stirring. As Duff watched, the feathers appeared to be lifting up, as if it were going to fly right at him. "Ahhhhh!" Duff screamed, his exclamation confirming what other onlookers had also seen.

"Great Caesar's ghost!" one man shouted, pointing straight at the crown. "It's alive! The peacock is alive!"

More screams erupted, frightening Duff into a corner. He held his head with both hands and shivered.

"The curse, the Guardian curse is real!" a woman shrieked. The room exploded with people running in all directions, frantically trying to escape.

Duff counted to five in his head, readying himself to make a run for the stairs so he could find Danny and Peachy. "Two, three, four," he prepared himself for the charge. "Five!" he yelled, rushing forward and smashing into a table. Globs of pudding splattered all over, and silverware flew in all directions. Duff struggled to free himself from a tablecloth that had somehow wrapped around his legs.

Feeling the threat of the peacock curse growing

closer, Duff lifted himself and the entire oak table up from the floor. Pumping his legs and arms like a runaway steam locomotive, he charged forward again, this time colliding head-on with a waiter. Man and boy both collapsed on the marble floor. Duff had another moment to be afraid before he felt his consciousness slip away.

———

Danny and Peachy, pressed together as if connected at the shoulder, tiptoed behind the waiter into the blackness that presided over the basement. With the serving man carrying only a single candle, the room was damp and dark.

"How come all you have is candles?" Peachy complained as the man lit one more of the feeble lights and handed it to Peachy.

"'Cause they've got all the lanterns up there, see?" Then rudely the waiter jeered, "Do you want your mommy, little muck snipe?" He ruffled Peachy's hair.

"Leave off!" Peachy demanded, jerking his head out of reach.

"All right then, shut your gob and do as I say." The man stopped in front of a double-sided wine rack that stretched the length of the low-arching brick ceiling for fifty feet or more. "You two take this row, and follow it all the way down to the end."

"But you haven't told us what we're looking for," Danny voiced, shaking his head.

The man rolled his eyes as if the boys were impossibly ignorant. "There's a gray electrical box somewhere on one of these walls. In it are all the fuses and the main switches for the lights and lifts. Now cut along. I don't want this to take all night."

The waiter turned away to start down the row, and Peachy stuck out his tongue and blew a loud, ripe raspberry. The waiter pretended not to notice.

"I feel the same way," Danny muttered. "Wonder if he gets paid to be a mug or if he lords it over us 'cause somebody else always lords it over him."

Both boys followed the retreating gleam of the candle. As it moved down the corridor, the glow illuminated a suspended stain of water on the ceiling. A single drop fell, splashing into a puddle on the bricks. They watched through the green glass bottles in the wine rack as the flame grew smaller and smaller. Another drop hit the floor, then the silence was broken by a rhythmic spurt of three more drops, then silence again.

"Oy, Danny. Look at this," Peachy said, holding a candle up to some old paintings.

The thick layers of paint were cracked wide in places and peeling in others. Peachy took a step back with the candle to get a better view. His movement revealed a young woman in a fluffy white dress and pearl earrings sitting on a rock in the countryside. Although she was beautiful, there was something eerie about her pale gray complexion. She appeared to have been either very sick or already dead when painted. It made the hair on Danny's neck stand up, and he looked away, just in time to hear another drop hit the puddle.

"This place reminds me of the caves near Bristol," Danny said, changing the subject. "Does it you?"

"That it does." Peachy recalled the time when he and Danny and Duff had visited the thirty-nine-chamber limestone caverns which stretched through an entire mountain. "And remember the furry bats that were right above your head, and how you accidentally burned them with your lantern?"

"Ahh, Peachy, I told you not to remind me of that," Danny said, looking unhappily nervous. "You know I hate bats."

"Don't worry, mate. I'm sure there aren't any down here."

"What makes you so sure?" Danny asked as they began walking slowly.

"It's the wine," Peachy answered confidently. "Bats hate wine."

Danny considered the idea but concluded that it was probably just another one of Peachy's made-up stories. "I wonder how old they are anyway?"

"The bats?" Peachy asked.

"Don't be dotty! I mean these bottles of wine."

"I don't know," Peachy answered. "Does it mat . . ."

"Shhhh," Danny hushed him. "I think I heard something." Danny listened for the familiar drop. It came, once . . . twice . . . and again, but the third drip sounded muffled, almost as if did not quite reach the floor.

"What?" Peachy questioned, tugging on the back of Danny's uniform. "What is it?"

Danny listened a moment longer before answering. "Nothing I guess. Maybe just the thought of the caves brought back too many spooky memories."

"Ah, you were just having me on for bringing up the bats! Don't do that, Danny!" Now it was Peachy's turn to wish he could change the subject. "Wonder how old these bottles actually are. Here, hold this," he said, handing the candle to Danny.

Gently grabbing the neck of a bottle on a row just above his head, Peachy began to slide it out slowly.

Danny looked around to see if he could still spot the waiter's candle. Sure enough, there it was, flickering faintly, off in the distance at the other end of the basement.

Peachy held the bottle closer and blew on it. Years of thick dust poured off, dropping heavily on the wet bricks. He further cleaned the label with his hand. "It says 1822." He paused a moment to think about it.

"Crikey," Danny remarked. "That *is* old."

"I'll bet it's really sour," Peachy predicted.

Danny gave a sudden cry that made Peachy turn sharply. Danny's face had lost all color and turned a pale, cold white like the girl in the painting. "The waiter's candle," he mumbled.

"What?" Peachy said looking in the direction he'd last seen it. "I said don't have me on, Danny. Not down here. I can't see anything. Cripes, what's that smell?"

"It just went out," Danny replied.

"Sulfur," Peachy answered his own question. "Maybe he turned the corner."

"No, I saw his candle fall to the ground."

Peachy shuddered, and his reddish hair stood up behind his ears. "Daniel," he whispered, "I think there's someone else down here."

Danny listened carefully. "How do you know?" he whispered back.

"That smell . . . sulfur . . . it smells like those lucifer matches; you know, the strong ones that you can light in the rain."

"Peachy, I didn't see anyone light any matches down here," Danny said softly. "Maybe we're both getting glocky. We'd better put that bottle up."

"I think you're right," Peachy agreed as he struggled to find the spot to replace the wine bottle. "Blimey, if we aren't a fine pair, talkin' ourselves into being scared! Help me, Danny. I can't see where this goes."

Danny lifted the candle high, but it was too late. Peachy had clumsily pushed the bottle roughly into what he thought was right place, but it shoved another out the other side.

Peachy and Danny both strained to grab the dislodged container, but they missed. At the moment the boys raised themselves on their toes, something moved on the other side of the rack. A creature or some animal spun around fast. Its eyes locked on theirs in a baneful stare that glowed green through the glass of the wine flasks.

The bottle hit the ground and shattered with a crash, and the boys let out violent screams. In a frantic struggle to escape the evil glare, they slipped and slid backward, knocking over a portrait of King Henry the Eighth. Still squirming, Danny and Peachy fought to climb out of the antique frame, smashing it to splinters in the process. "Blimey!" Peachy shouted. "We're for it now!" Back down the long hall they ran, shoving aside crates, boxes, and paintings.

A mere ten feet from the stairs, which beckoned with the promise of safety and escape, a tall silhouette stepped out to block their path. "He's there!" Peachy yelled, skidding to a stop so quickly that Danny plowed into him from behind.

The two friends yelled again as they staggered, stumbled, and fell on the slick paving. "Boys," a concerned voice called down to them, "what's the matter?"

Danny slowly opened his eyes and raised them. Peachy shook his head in a violent negative; it did not sound like the voice of a monster, but it could be a trap. The man spoke again. "I just came down to check on the lights, when I heard you boys scream. Are you all right?" He hung a lantern from a hook set in a wooden beam.

The voice sound slightly familiar, Danny thought. When he looked at the smiling face, he recognized the man as having been on the platform at the dinner.

As if guessing his thought, the man said, "I'm Patrick Gannon. This old basement is a spooky place, eh what? Especially with the old forged paintings stored down here. It's enough to give anybody the willies."

Realizing they were safe, the boys clambered to their feet. "Mr. Gannon," Danny exclaimed, "over there we saw someone watching us through the rack, and the waiter's gone, and . . ."

"What, what?" Gannon said with a laugh. "Slow down."

Danny began again, more slowly this time. "We were down here with a waiter to find the switch box, and we started looking around, when we noticed his candle had gone out."

"Down this wine rack," Peachy joined in, "I was looking at this bottle, and then this pair of green eyes was staring back at me."

"Show me where," Gannon suggested, ushering them down the corridor.

"No, sir," Danny shook his head. "I don't want to go back down there."

"Oh, come now," Gannon urged. "Don't be afraid. I'm with you."

Peachy considered the fact that Mr. Gannon was an adult, and a pretty good-sized one at that. "Right-o, but you lead the way."

"Fair enough," Gannon agreed, pulling out a box of matches from his pocket to light the lanterns spaced along the walls.

"Right there," Peachy said, pointing to the empty spot on the wine rack.

Walking directly to it, Gannon held up a match. "Oh yes, I see. Look here. The backs of the bottles are round and curved inward. I can see how candlelight and the mind's tricks when one is scared could make this look like a pair of eyes."

Danny stepped up to take a peek. Sure enough, the wavy glass bottoms reflecting the match flame did look like a pair of eyes.

Gannon quickly pulled the curling match away to blow it out. He turned slowly while striking another one, then lit an additional lantern.

"Here is a gray box," Danny announced, indicating a metal container hung on the wall. "Is this what we're looking for?"

"Quite right," Gannon agreed as he opened up the small door to the panel. "Amazing stuff, this electricity. Not got all the bugs worked out of it yet, to my thinking."

Something made a groaning sound farther down the

dark corridor. Peachy and Danny froze again and looked back toward the stairs while Gannon squinted to see what made the sound.

"Oh, my head," the voice of the waiter complained from somewhere in the dark reaches of the basement.

The server staggered out of the blackness, holding his hand to his forehead. When he took his palm down, there was a bloody stain above his right eye.

"Did someone hit you?" Gannon asked.

"No, I don't think so," the battered waiter recalled. "I fell and hit my head. But I think someone tripped me."

"You probably just stumbled in the dark," Gannon said. "It seems rather easy to come to grief down here tonight. But here's something odd," he added, studying the electrical panel.

"What?" Peachy and Danny demanded with one voice.

"The fuse hasn't blown after all. The main switch is turned off." Gannon pushed a two-pronged handle from down to up, and a small light above the box came on. At the same instant they could hear the motor of the newly installed electric lift warming up in a whining hum.

Another light appeared just a few feet away in an elevator shaft which the boys had not even realized was there. With a clank as the cables engaged the winding drums, Danny, Peachy, Gannon, and the waiter heard the car of the lift speed up the shaft to the floor above.

———

The electric lights of the British Museum blinked several times, with long intervals of darkness in between.

The flickering bulbs seemed to be contemplating whether they would turn on again.

When the fixtures finally did relight to stay, the once beautiful banquet hall was not a pretty sight. Tables were overturned, and food was everywhere. The stone face of Tiglath-Pilezer wore a coating of crème caramel, and coffee dripped from the basalt nose of Sennacherib. Most of the guests got up to leave, forming an enormous line at the cloak check. It would probably take thirty minutes to complete the recovery of top hats and canes.

Still lying on the floor, half-conscious, Duff pinned the little waiter down. Duff's limp body lay over the man like the statue of an ancient Greek wrestler in a crushing victory.

The distinctive throbbing whine of the lift machinery roused the boy at last. The lift chugged its way up to the level of the Assyrian Salon, but Duff was still too groggy to move.

Douglas Macintire reappeared at the podium. He announced his apologies for the disastrous event that had overtaken dinner. In front of him, still sealed in its glass cage, was the Jewelled Peacock Crown. Its tail remained spread in a circlet of shimmering gold. Just the sight of it had made hundreds shiver in fear and had wrecked an entire banquet. Tomorrow the bizarre happenings would be on the front page of every paper in London.

Danny and Peachy led the way up the stairs from the cellar. Rounding the last corner from the Nimrod Gallery, they reentered the dining hall. "What happened here?" Danny asked in disbelief. "We leave for ten minutes, and the whole place has gone topsy-turvy."

Peachy chuckled. "We thought it was rough down

there. Blimey! If I started a shindy with one bottle, I'd like to know how many bottles they pulled out to make this come about!"

Danny laughed. Shaking his head at the chaos, he spotted Duff lying on the floor, covered in crockery and pudding. "Look, there's Duff." Danny made his way toward their friend, passing a table where a woman complained to her husband in disgust, "I can't believe I let you drag me to one of these wretched Persian Society dinners. Was that supposed to be some kind of a joke?"

"But dear," the man argued, "they're not all like this."

The scandalized woman flicked her silk scarf around her throat and said, "I'm never doing this again." She walked off, her nose pointing skyward, leaving her husband to tag along behind, pleading for forgiveness.

The next table Danny and Peachy passed had several older couples around it. An extremely tall, thin man, with a pencil-line moustache, announced in a self-righteous tone, "I've never seen the like of it! The nerve of them bringing that kind of evil into the room after they *knew* about the curse. I'm surprised they didn't bring the devil himself."

Danny heard a younger, scholarly gentleman announce, "Do you know how much publicity this will draw? The society used to be called stuffy! Well, no more! This thing was big, and I saw it, the whole disaster, right here."

Overhearing the talk at the different tables built a picture in Danny's mind about what had happened. *The scholar was right,* he thought. No matter whether frightened, thrilled, or disgusted, no one left the evening uninterested or bored. Every one of them, and thousands of other readers, would be fascinated by the story in tomorrow's news. Word of this occurrence would even spread from London to the whole of England and the Continent. Within a day it would be spoken of in America. *News,* Danny concluded, *makes the world go 'round.*

"Duff, are you all right?" Danny shook the prostrate boy's shoulder and patted his face, trying to revive him. "Peachy, grab some water, would you?"

"Right-o, mate."

Beneath Duff's bulk, the little waiter gasped for a breath of air. "Get this lug off me!" he panted. Peachy returned with a glass of water, sloshing some on Duff's face.

With a groan Duff attempted to climb off the man. Slow and shaky, the boy slipped on the sauce-soaked carpet and fell back to the floor, crushing the waiter again. If the man had managed one good breath, it was all squeezed out of him once more. He was left wheezing and rolling his eyes.

Peachy and Danny each grabbed one of Duff's arms, helping him to his feet. Duff looked fearfully around the room, blinking in the light.

"What happened here, Duff?" Danny questioned, brushing some of the chunks of porcelain and globs of pudding off Duff's uniform.

"I, I . . . I don't kn-know," Duff stuttered. "The p-p-peacock spooked the whole room."

"What? How did it do that, Duff?" Peachy demanded, grabbing Duff's arm. "Duff Bernard, how did the crown spook the room?" he repeated.

Duff opened his mouth, but no words came out. His

eyes took on a far-off look, as if he were somewhere else. Danny and Peachy tried to get his attention, waving a hand in front of him, shaking him, even throwing more water in his face, but nothing worked.

Peachy looked worried. "Do you think he'll be all right, Danny?"

"I think so. He's probably just in shock from whatever happened. I'm sure he'll be back to normal once we get him out of here."

Just then, a shrill scream howled from the lift. "A snake! I've been bitten by a snake!"

This new alarm captured the attention of everyone in the room. All eyes and heads turned toward the lift as an elderly gentlemen hobbled out of the metal cage. He groaned, grasped his chest, then fell face first to the ground.

In the back of the lift, what seemed to be a short length of dirty brown rope recoiled itself on the floor. The dusky snake hissed and struck at its own image reflected in the polished wall.

Patrick Gannon ran to the lift. "Quick," he called to the boys, "throw me that bowl!"

Diving forward, Danny gripped the handle of a fancy silver serving bowl and yanked it from the table. Figs and plums from the after-dinner fruit offering bounced on the chairs as Danny slid the container across the floor. The bowl slowed to a stop just in front of the lift door.

Gannon licked his lips and swallowed hard. The snake was within striking distance of the bowl. To reach it Gannon would have to expose himself to its obviously deadly bite.

Danny saw beads of sweat appear on the man's forehead. Gannon slowly reached for the bowl while holding onto the brass framed door. The snake coiled tighter and watched the man's every move.

When Gannon's hand was a single inch from touching the bowl, the deadly serpent reared back its head, then struck at his arm. Gannon grabbed the container by its base and flung it powerfully at the reptile.

The snake collided with the heavy dish and was knocked backward. Gannon slammed the lift door shut as the bowl wobbled to a stop, halfway covering the viper. The reptile found the bowl to be a cozy den and slowly pulled in its tail until its entire body was under the silver dome. A tiny white fang lay broken off next to the bowl.

Those in the crowd who had not run screaming for the exits were impressed but dared not clap. Lying on the floor of the salon was the man who had been bitten. The earl of Shaftsbury felt for a pulse in the man's neck, then shook his head sadly.

Gannon stood and wiped his forehead. "It was meant for me," he said shakily. "It's the curse . . ."

Douglas Macintire shushed him hurriedly. The American was all business. "Send to the Zoological Society for a snake keeper," he ordered. "Have them send someone to collect the animal."

The remaining guests stampeded out, dodging velvet ropes and looking sideways at drapery pulls. Every shadow under every chair might harbor another viper!

Danny mentally reviewed the evening's events. The power outage, the crown with its curse, and now the lift with the snake, resulting in the death of a man. He turned to Peachy and said, "I think we've got a case."

THREE

BAKER STREET was bustling with activity when the boys rounded the corner from Marylebone High Street. Hansom cabs jostled for position with freight wagons, delivery vans, and double-decker omnibuses. Draft horses moved in and out of the scene, leaving behind aromatic reminders of their passing.

All of this action was going on just in front of the London residence of the famous consulting detective, Mr. Sherlock Holmes. Something at the window of Holmes's place, 221B, caught Peachy's eye. "Blimey, Danny. Ain't that smoke coming from Mr. Holmes's window?"

It certainly was. A stream of black fumes was soaring upward from the second story. A moment later there was more than just vapor emerging from the window. As the boys ran forward, a ladder-back oak chair crashed through the glass, taking out both upper and lower panes. The shattered window tinkled down on the sidewalk harmlessly, but the chair sailed over the street and landed with a clatter on top of a passing police van. The horses neighed, rearing and plunging, as the driver sawed at the reins.

"Crikey!" Danny exclaimed. "It nailed that Black Maria! Come on! Mr. Holmes must be in a terrible fight for his life!"

"Too right!" Peachy agreed. "Charge, Duff! Holmes is in a right dustup!"

Upon reaching the outskirts of the gathering crowd, Danny smelled a sulphurous odor. "Uh-oh! It smells like one of Mr. Holmes's experiments."

Duff pushed up behind them, but a pair of bobbies of the Metropolitan Police Force were already hammering on the door. The same concern for the sleuth's safety had occurred to them, for they were shouting, "Mr. 'Olmes, are you all right? Open up, sir, if you please."

Peachy grabbed Danny, who grabbed Duff, and the three threaded their way through the mob. Then they heard Holmes's voice. "Ladies and gentlemen, I assure you there is nothing amiss here. I am fine. No cause for alarm."

One of the constables continued to stand at the door, while the other bobby climbed up on top of the paddy wagon and removed the chair. When the front door opened at last, the first officer fired off a load of questions at the famous detective. But Holmes merely accepted the return of his chair, said thank you, and shut his door. The two policemen exchanged looks of consternation. Because there was no harm done and the detective was obviously all right, they urged the crowd to break it up, and then they departed as well.

"Watch this," Peachy said to Danny. He went

straight up to the door and rapped loudly with the knocker. "Mr. Holmes, open this door immediately!" he barked in a gruff voice.

"Come in, Carnehan!" Holmes shouted from within.

"Aw, Mr. Holmes, how did you know it was me?" Peachy said as he opened the heavy door. He looked disappointed.

"Elementary, lad," Holmes called from upstairs. "Your voice is naturally in a register higher than an adult voice. When an attempt is made at lowering the pitch, certain dual tones are generated, ruining . . ."

Peachy interrupted him. "Fine, fine. My blinking voice cracks."

"Correct," Holmes said simply as the group reached the first floor landing. "Now about this peacock affair."

Danny's jaw dropped in amazement. He was about to ask how Holmes knew the reason for their visit but thought better of it. "Yes, Mr. Holmes," he acknowledged, "that's why we came . . . but wait! What about all the smoke and smell fuming out of this place?"

"Ah, very good Wiggins," Holmes exclaimed. "Never let yourself be distracted when investigating. The suspect should never run the show." Peachy rolled his eyes. "It just happens that Mrs. Hudson is away in the Scottish Highlands on family business, and I merely overcooked my supper."

Danny laughed and said, "What about the window then?"

"Oh, that has needed to be fixed for some time. It just wouldn't open adequately to ventilate the smoke. I took the most expedient method available." Holmes saw the amused looks on the boys' faces. "What would you have me do? Suffocate up here?"

Danny and Peachy began rolling with laughter. Even Duff, who did not understand the joke, started chuckling.

"Now," Holmes said, attempting to regain control of the situation, "about this Persian crown. I know what you've come to ask, but there's really no mystery here, boys."

Peachy was not content to leave Holmes in possession of unexplained supernatural powers. "But how *did* you know we came about the crown?"

"Uncomplicated logic. I read the *Times* today in which residents of the Waterloo Road School were listed as having been witnesses to the, quote 'extraordinary events of last evening.' Actually, the events are rather bland and boring. I think even Scotland Yard should be able to catch the culprits. In any case, I not only knew what you wanted, I have been expecting your visit."

"Well, who is it then?" Peachy demanded.

"None other than a Persian cult known as the Guardians of the Peacock. They are the sworn protectors of the sacred Persian treasures and the enemies of British influence in their homeland. If they cannot regain the crown, embarrassing this country with poppycock nonsense about mysterious spells will serve their ends both here and at home. I'm sure with a little bit of luck, even Lestrade will be able to put an end to this so-called curse."

I hope so, Danny thought, *without Holmes on the case . . .*

"Now be off, boys," Holmes said, ushering them downstairs. "I've some cleaning to do."

The Baker Street Brigade left 221B. Danny felt as though something were missing in the case, something he could not quite bring to mind. "Say, Peachy, doesn't it feel strange that Holmes has this case all figured out?"

"No," Peachy said simply, idly kicking a fragment of broken glass into the gutter. "Mr. Holmes knows what he's talking about."

"I know Mr. Holmes knows what he's doing," Danny insisted. "It just feels like something's missing."

"I have all my things," Duff said, patting his pockets.

"What?" Peachy shot him a funny look.

"No, Duff," Danny said, "I meant something isn't right with this whole peacock thing."

"Cap'n Mewsley says there's snakes in Africa could swallow whole peacock things," Duff said in reference to their friend who was in charge of the newspaper boys in central London. Duff stared off into the distance as if seeing the heart of a jungle instead of Regents Park.

"That's it!" Danny exclaimed, stopping in midstep. Duff almost knocked him down from behind.

"What's it?" Peachy asked, sounding annoyed.

"Why, the snake, of course!" Danny said. "Would the Guardian faction, or whatever they're called, bring a snake with them from Persia?"

"Danny, there's no mystery here," Peachy countered. "They're a bunch of loonies. A better question is what other horrible things they brought from Persia. They *want* people to be scared."

"Yes, but couldn't they get a snake from . . ." Danny looked up and pointed at the road sign indicating Regents Park and the London Zoological Society.

"C'mon, Peachy," Danny announced with growing excitement. "I know where our next clue will be."

"Wait, Danny! Slow down," Peachy pleaded. "How do you expect to get in with no money? We can't just tell them we're investigating a case for Sherlock Holmes."

Danny looked suddenly glum. He and Peachy turned out the insides of their pockets and discovered a total of sixpence between them.

"I know who has money," Duff said. "Clair has lots of money."

"That's no good, Duff," Danny said. "We can't just go get Clair so she can pay our way for us. I have some in my mattress at school. We can use it."

"Are you crazy, Danny?" Peachy said. "You were saving that money for something important, not for an afternoon at the zoo."

"This is important to me," Danny said. "Now, c'mon, let's go get it."

———

Duff heaved open the giant oak door to the Ragged School and held it for his friends.

"You and Peachy stay here, Duff," Danny said as he walked through. "I'll be right down."

When Danny had gone around the first corner of the old staircase inside, Peachy said, "I can't believe he's going to waste his money on the zoo."

"Hullo, Clair," Duff said, looking over Peachy's shoulder.

"Cor, I wish," Peachy said. "But you're not going to make me turn around with that old trick."

"Hello, Duffer," a sweet voice came from behind

Peachy. He swung around, snatching off his cap and hastily running his hand over his unruly hair.

"Clair!" Peachy exclaimed, his voice cracking. "What're you doing here?"

"It's nice to see you too, Peachy Carnehan. Where's Danny?"

Clair Avery, daughter of Inspector Avery of Scotland Yard, lived in a different world from that of the orphans of the Waterloo Road Ragged School. Yet she was almost a member of the Brigade. She could get information from places where the street slang and much-mended clothing of the boys would have gotten them thrown out.

"He's inside," Peachy stammered. "He's going to get . . . something."

Clair smiled. "I read the paper today, and it said that you were witnesses to what happened at the museum. Aren't you working on this case? I'm surprised you haven't come for my help."

"Cripes," Peachy said, rolling his eyes. "Does anyone *not* know our business?"

"What?" Clair asked, looking confused.

"Never mind. Look, Danny's gone to fetch some money, and we're going to the zoo to granny the snake. No doubt you read about that too." Clair nodded. Then shyly Peachy added, "You can come along, if you want."

Just then Danny appeared back in the doorway to the school. "Clair, what're you doing here?"

"If that's all you gentlemen can say to me, I can leave!"

"No, uh, sorry. It's just such a surprise to see you. We were just on our way to the . . ."

"I know, I've already been invited."

At the gate of the reptile house in the London Zoo, Duff paused. "I don't much feel like it," he remarked to himself.

"What'd you say, Duff?" Danny asked.

Duff shook his head slowly from side to side. "I don't want to go into the snake place," he said. "I seen the snake last night. I don't like 'em."

"That's okay, Duff," Danny reassured his friend. "You just wait right out here." Danny, Peachy, and Clair entered under the clock tower of the brick building into the semidarkness of the reptile house.

Danny stared in awe down the long hall, lined on both sides with hundreds of glass cases. Besides snakes from all over the world, there were lizards, crocodiles, snapping turtles, and toads.

The cages were backed with thin wooden planks, drilled with hundreds of tiny holes for air. Behind these Danny could see walkways where food and supplies were kept.

"I'd be happy to help you with any queth-shuns that you have," a soft voice called from the far end of the dimly lit enclosure. The words echoed strangely in the building, and at first Danny could not distinguish where the speaker was located.

Clair saw him first. "Thank you very much," she said, as a dark-skinned man wearing a turban approached them.

Danny thought the man looked East Indian. He was wearing thick, stiff leather gloves that covered his arms to the elbows.

"We'd like to see the snake that they brought here

from the museum dinner," Clair said politely. Danny had warned her not to say anything about their investigation. "We're curious," she added. "We read about it in the paper."

The man had a plump face and dark eyes that were sunken behind a small nose. "Oh, yeth," he lisped. "A very fine th-nake indeed. Not to look at, no. Very plain, very common in form. But curiouth in manner and activity. Come, let me tell you."

Peachy snickered at the reptile keeper's snakelike accent, but an angry glance from Clair made him keep it to himself.

The group followed the man down the corridor to a cage near the opposite entrance to the reptile house. The case was on the bottom row, and Peachy examined it closely to avoid looking at the snake keeper and laughing again.

There in the pen, nearly invisible on its branch, lay the snake the boys had glimpsed the night before. The keeper was right; it was unremarkable in appearance. Small and brown, it had neither bright colors nor rattles to warn of its venom. "That's it," Peachy concluded. "Doesn't look scary in there, does it?"

"Indeed, no, by Jove," agreed the snake keeper. "A hearth viper. Very plain. Little and brown. Good color for hiding in ith native region."

"Where is it from?" Clair asked. This was the key issue about which they wanted information.

"The hearth viper can be found anywhere from the Thahara in Africa, all the way to India. More people die each year from the bite of the hearth viper than any other th-nake in the world."

"Why is that?" Danny asked.

"It will coil in the dirt floor of the native hut to cool off. Then it ith very hard to th-ee. Not a predator, by Jove, but it will th-trike the unfortunate on the bare feet." The friends cringed at the thought of being bitten in such a tender spot. "Not the mo-th deadly venom in the world but found very commonly where there are native hut-th, you th-ee?"

Danny bent down to examine the snake through the protective glass. So far they had not learned anything useful. This particular snake might have come from Persia or it might not. It was as big around as Danny's thumb and perhaps two feet long. It had looked bigger in the lift—more frightening too. Its flat, black eyes appeared unseeing, set in a small head. In fact the only way Danny could tell it was alive was by the small forked tongue that would dart from the mouth every few seconds to taste the air around it.

Now, Danny thought, *how did you get in the lift? And why? If only you could talk.*

"Would you like to th-ee it nearer?" the reptile keeper asked.

Peachy shook his head and stepped back. "Not me, mate," he refused. "This is as close as I want to get."

Danny and Clair were very interested, however. "Definitely," Clair said. The snake keeper walked away and in a moment reappeared behind the enclosures. He knelt on the floor next to the case and slid the door open about an inch. Distracting the snake by scratching on the pen at the opposite end, he quickly reached in and grabbed the snake just behind the head.

"How do you handle them so well?" Danny asked in astonishment when the man returned.

The keeper shrugged. "Many year-th of work. You recall what I explained?" he asked, holding the animal up. "Very plain, but deadly becau-th of it." He forced the reptile's mouth open. The snake extended its fangs, and Danny could see the remainder of the one that had broken at the dinner. The snake keeper seemed to notice it also.

"What happened here?" he asked, lifting the snake to eye level. "I did not know they damaged you in capture. Thi-th will not do at all." He held the snake mere inches from his own face, and Danny envisioned the viper wriggling free and lashing out.

The man continued to talk to the group while staring at the reptile. "Deadly enough. Only one in one hundred people will live after being bitten by a hearth viper. I have been bitten twelve time-th by them. Death can take up to a week. The victim will immediately black out, then begin to dream weirdly. Extreme fever follow-th."

He spoke in low tones directly to the snake, almost as if the group of children were no longer standing in front of him. "Pain beyond belief. The hand-th of the victim curl uncontrollably inward, driving the nail-th into the palm-th." He clenched his left fist at his side and closed his eyes. "Frightening. A horrible nightmare from which I couldn't awake . . ." He suddenly changed the subject. "However, thith particular animal ith no threat. It hath no venom pouch. Either malformed at birth or removed."

The group was struck speechless by the man's tale of his narrow escape from horrible death. Finally Danny found the nerve to speak. "That's strange. The papers all reported that the man who was bitten died of the snake's lethal poison."

Behind the group, Peachy heard someone enter the work area behind the cages at the opposite end of the hall. The snake keeper dropped the snake to waist level, still holding its jaws wide open. "Well, children, I will be off." He headed for the door. "By the way, did it note in the newthpaper that the th-nake would be brought here to the reptile house?"

"Yes, sir," Danny said, "but I was also there when it was captured and heard someone say it."

"Ah . . . very well. Good day."

"Wait, please," Clair called after him. "What is your name?"

The snake handler stopped in the doorway. "Rajeev Goa."

"Thank you, Mr. Goa," Danny said. "You've been very helpful."

"My job," he said with a bow, and with that he was gone.

Outside, Peachy laughed uncontrollably. "Did you hear that loon? Blimey, you sure can tell he's not lying about those snakebite-th." He added a lisp to the end of the word to mimic Goa's speech impediment.

"Peachy Carnehan," Clair scolded, "how can you be so cruel? He is a nice, helpful man, who probably suffers from being made fun of."

Just then Duff walked up to the group. "Hullo," he said simply.

Danny looked at him thoughtfully. "Hi, Duff," he said. "We can go home to supper now." Turning back to

Peachy, Danny said, "It's the same thing, Peachy . . . the same as if you laughed at Duff here."

"Oh, give over," Peachy said. "I didn't mean nothing by it."

"I'm funny sometimes," Duff agreed. Clair patted him on the back and he smiled.

FOUR

LATER THAT NIGHT, inside the darkened, brooding hulk of the British Museum, guards patrolled the grounds. The tapping of boot heels clicked rhythmically, almost hypnotically, as the sentries made their rounds. Each guard walked in a measured pace so as to keep precisely the same distance between his fellow watchmen. Sometimes a man would catch a glimpse of the warden ahead as he turned the widely spaced corners. More than one guard wondered if he were really all alone in the echoing halls, the fleeting image ahead only a mirage.

Such a thought occurred to Watchman Bristol. After twelve years with the Metropolitan Police Force, a fall from a second-story window had forced his retirement as a bobby. He had caught on immediately at the museum, but now, three years later, he was still unused to the eerie silence.

After tapping up several steps, Bristol's path turned left into the Asiatic Room. A twelfth-century gilded statue of Buddha towered over the rest of the exhibits.

The figure always seemed to Bristol to be looking at him when he entered the hall and still watching as he left it.

In the hall was a staircase which led down to the library, but Bristol went up instead. At the top of a few more steps sat another guard, old Hubert. Hubert never bothered to say cheerio; the bloke was always asleep anyway.

Bristol passed through the long wing of Ethnographical Studies and entered the North Gallery. The North Gallery was always the worst for giving a man a sudden chill. The flickering light of his bull's-eye lantern barely illuminated the side rooms containing Egyptian tomb paintings. The dancing beams made the halls seem like real crypts along the Nile River.

And if the eyes of the long-dead people in the paintings were not bad enough, the next gallery was the Egyptian Mummy Room. Some of the dried-up corpses were displayed in tattered bandages. Some were still in wooden sarcophagi which dated back thousands of years, though still perfectly preserved. Bristol could never decide which was worse: the horrid grimaces on the faces of the partly unwrapped cadavers or the suspicion that a wooden lid might lift at any moment to reveal something even more terrifying.

Bristol frowned as he passed the door of Douglas Macintire's office. That American had enough brass to be a ship captain. Macintire practically ran the place, giving orders as if he were the curator of the museum instead of an invited guest. Bristol wondered if all Americans were so annoying.

Just as Bristol pivoted on his heel to descend to the northwest landing, he heard a sudden noise inside Macintire's office. The watchman quickly covered the lens of his lantern and stopped to listen.

———————

Inside Douglas Macintire's office, light from the gas streetlamp outside the window cast a dim silver glow on the furniture. The desk had been left neat and clean, as was the rest of the office.

Behind the desk on the floor was the submerged heating channel. Its outlets covered with smooth brass grates, the heating channel was about one foot wide and contained the steam pipes from the immense boiler in the subbasement. The channels ran from room to room under all the floors and served as the heat source for the entire museum. Of course, in the warmth of midsummer the fires in the furnace were out and the pipes cold.

Seconds after Watchman Bristol's footsteps passed the door, fingers reached upward through the diamond-shaped holes of the brass grate. Clenching the cool metal tightly, a pair of muscularly corded arms raised a section of the grate and slid it quietly to the side. A dark figure climbed out of the heating channel.

Carefully navigating around the desk, the shadowy form picked up a candle from a shelf near the door. The intruder drew a box of matches from his pocket. He struck one against a fragment of ancient pottery on a shelf. The flaring yellow flame revealed a desert-darkened face. He lit the candle, then dropped the match into the saucer of the candleholder. The splinter of glowing wood died down to a dull cherry on the end of a curling black stem. A miniature spiral of smoke slithered upward like a thin, inky snake.

Searching the desk, the man pulled out every desk drawer and dumped its contents. Finding nothing, he looked on shelves and under tables, even pulled pictures from the walls. The Persian grunted with frustration.

Suddenly the man started as he spotted the small bookshelf behind Macintire's desk. The dark figure hurried over to the oak cupboard and wiggled it from side to side.

———

Watchman Bristol checked his pocket watch. The next sentry would be coming soon. He sniffed a faint whiff of smoke in the air. When he silently tried the doorknob of Macintire's office, he found it securely locked.

Tiptoeing back to meet the oncoming sentry, Bristol placed the man in front of the door with instructions to remain silent. Meanwhile, Bristol went to report.

"Captain," Bristol saluted, "upon minute ten of my last round I heard a noise and smelled smoke in Douglas Macintire's office. Is he in late, sir?"

"I'll check," the captain replied, scanning the page of his clearance ledger. "Did you knock?"

"No, sir," Bristol answered. "You know how angry that American gentleman gets if he's disturbed."

"He's not checked in," the captain concluded, looking up. "You say it was smoke you smelled?"

"Yes, particularly strong sulfur," Bristol replied, "like from a newly lit match."

The captain grabbed the master ring of keys and made his way back toward Macintire's office with Bristol.

"Ah," the Persian intruder snorted angrily, unable to find a hidden catch and still trying to pull the bookshelf away from the wall. A small rug scooted out from under the Persian's feet, and he knocked loose a shelf. Books and geographic journals spilled as the man crashed hard onto the wooden floor. As he looked around the room to regain his bearings, he noticed something shiny on the floor where the carpet used to be. It was a safe, sunken flush with the floor. The office door rattled suddenly, and fists pounded on the panel.

The Persian man scurried to replace the rug. He hurried to the window to unlatch it, then blew out the candle. The burglar climbed back into the heating channel seconds before the key turned in the lock.

The oak door slammed against the wall as it opened. The light of three lanterns streamed in just as the bandit pulled the grate back over his head. It settled in place with barely a rattle.

"Look, Captain," Bristol said, pointing to the still smoldering candle. "Someone's been here and just left."

"Check the window," the captain ordered.

"It's unlocked."

The captain blew the discordant police whistle as loudly as he could. Additional guards came running from both directions.

A finger tapped the shoulder of Chief Inspector Avery. He was sitting with his daughter, Clair, in the darkened Lyric Theater, just blocks away from the museum. The overture music was being played, and the curtain was about to raise on Gilbert and Sullivan's *H.M.S. Pinafore.* Avery looked up to see a uniformed guard of the British Museum standing behind him. "Inspector Avery," the guard whispered, "there's been a robbery. Inspector Lestrade told me to find you here and ask that you come immediately."

Avery replied with irritation, "What's so important that I'm to be pulled away from this time with my daughter?"

"It's the Peacock Crown, sir. We've arrested a Persian who broke in to steal it."

Realizing the significance of the guard's statement, Avery sighed. "Just one minute." He needed to figure out what to say to Clair. They had been looking forward to this outing for a month. Ever since the death of Clair's mother, he had made special efforts to be together with his daughter. The chief inspector leaned over and whispered in his daughter's ear. "Clair, my child, there's been a robbery attempt at the museum, and I'm called to go at once."

"But, Father!" she exclaimed in disappointment.

"I know," he replied, "but this must be really important, or they wouldn't send the men after me here."

Clair thought about the British Museum and the Baker Street Brigade and the reptile man. A butterfly flew through her stomach as she realized there might be a connection between this burglary and last night's events. Formulating a plan, she turned with girlish charm. "But, Father, I don't want to go home now."

"Very well, I'll have a cab take you home after the program."

"I don't want to go home alone." She gave her father the saddest look she knew.

"Well, then," he said, trying to make it up to her. "Why don't you come with me to see what's happened?"

Her response was short and simple: "Yes, Father."

Inspector Avery put on his hat, not knowing how he had been gulled. Clair followed him out of the theater, headed for danger, headed for excitement. With luck, she would be heading for the success of another case for the Baker Street Brigade.

The streets were damp from a summer thunderstorm, and the night was muggy. The carriage pulled into the curving drive that rounded up to the enormous museum structure. Inspector Lestrade came down to meet them.

Lestrade clapped his hands together. "Ah good, Chief Inspector, you made it. You are in time to watch the interrogation."

"Do you mean to say you have already solved the case?"

"Quite," Lestrade said grandly. "The perpetrator is in custody."

"So where is he?" Avery asked, getting right to the point.

"We've got him shackled, waitin' in the wagon just over there."

Avery was pleased and a little surprised at Lestrade's success. "Good work," he admitted. "Where was he captured?"

"In a ventilation shaft. He was hiding under the floor of Douglas Macintire's office and about to make his getaway. His pocket caught on a steam pipe, and in his struggle to free himself a matchbox ignited." Lestrade laughed. "He yelled and kicked something terrible until the men pulled him out, still smoldering!" Clair was only a single step behind her father, listening to every word.

"Really?" Avery sounded amused. "How droll! But how'd he get in?"

"I think he must have hidden somewhere in the museum before closing," Lestrade informed Avery, opening the door for his superior and Clair. "By the amount of dust on his clothes, I'd say he'd been climbing around a long time."

Avery mused, "Perhaps there will be a trail we can follow back to where he got into the heating channel. Put a man on it, Inspector. And see that the Persian fellow is taken to Old Bailey for questioning."

The Central Criminal Court, known as the Old Bailey, had had jurisdiction over criminal justice in London and its surrounding areas since the year 1539. Once a criminal was arrested and taken for questioning at the Old Bailey, escape was almost impossible. The Persian was in for a rough night.

The police carriage drove through the gate in the high walls that surrounded the prison. Though Clair had visited Old Bailey with her father on other occasions, she had never gotten used to the sounds and the smells. The odor drifting up from the below-ground cells made her hurriedly clap a perfume-soaked handkerchief to her nose. Still under construction, the new dome for the Old Bailey courts already towered 212 feet over Clair's head as she entered.

"Clair," Inspector Avery instructed, "you wait here while I get to the bottom of this." He showed her to a sitting room for court visitors. "If you need anything, Officer Richards over there at security will take care of you." Avery pointed to a round-faced redhead. Richards was overweight with a double-double chin, but he looked kind and grinned when he waved.

Clair smiled and waved back. "Yes, Father," she answered meekly. She peeked around the corner to see where her father went as he walked off. Avery turned left at the end of the hall. Clair listened as a door creaked open, then slammed shut. Then she heard the shuffling step and the jingle of chains as the shackled prisoner was brought in. She could not see him, but she knew her father was right down the hall. She had to find out what they were talking about.

Clair had an idea. She leaned forward to catch sight of Officer Richards. He was busy with some kind of paperwork.

"Excuse me, please," she called politely.

"Yes, miss, what can I do for you?"

"May I use the ladies room, please?" she asked in her most delicate voice.

"Well, we don't have one of those," he replied in a deep Welsh accent. "Don't get too many ladies around here. But you may use the magistrate's wash-up if you like. Follow me, I'll show you where it is."

He stood and she followed him toward where she already knew the lavatory was. As they went down the hall and passed the interrogation room, Clair slowed her pace. Sure enough, she caught a tiny bit of her father's voice saying something about the museum basement.

Richards opened up the door to a closet-sized room, squeezing through it as his belly and back touched either side. He twisted a brass light switch proudly. "Here you are, miss," he beamed. "Just turn off this electricity knob when you're finished."

"Thank you," she replied, shutting the door. The room contained a toilet with an overhead tank and pull chain and a single sink and faucet. Clair turned on the water for a few seconds to make it sound as if she were washing up.

Peeking out, she found that Richards had gone back to his desk. Gathering her courage, she snuck across the hall to where her father was.

With her ear to the door, Clair listened to the fragments of conversation. She could not hear the robber's responses, only her father's questions. His voice sounded angry. "So you are a member of the Guardian cult." There was a pause. "And your people are the ones that released a deadly snake." Clair listened carefully.

The man must have denied it, probably blaming it on the curse from the sound of her father's next response. "Ha! That won't wash, my man! Curse, indeed! I'll tell you why you did it: to create fear, panic, superstition! You murdered in hopes that the crown would be returned because of the curse!" he yelled. "You'd better give me straight answers, or you're for it. You'll hang!"

Clair shuddered. Then she remembered what the reptile keeper said: The snake had no poison. Could it still be murder even if the man had only placed a harmless snake in the museum?

A long pause followed in the interrogation room, then Clair heard her father say, "Charge him with murder and attempted robbery. He'll talk after a few nights in the hole."

Clair hurried back to the waiting area, waved to Richards, and sat down a split second before the door opened and her father emerged.

All the way home Clair worried about the Persian man in jail. Yet she was afraid to tell her father what the brigade had found out that day from the reptile keeper. Why had she not told him sooner? He sounded so angry and frustrated, and he would probably get even more upset if he found out she had been eavesdropping. The evening was ruined now, and she wished she had never known about the crown at all.

Then she brightened at another thought. If only the Baker Street Brigade could prove that the man in the museum had died of another cause, then the robber might not have to hang. She would have to contact Danny and Peachy first thing tomorrow.

FIVE

DANNY SAT bolt upright in bed early the next morning. He looked around the large bunk room of the Waterloo Road Ragged School. As near as he could guess, it was only six o'clock. Peachy would not wake for another two hours—just in time for chapel. Breakfast would not be served until nine on this Saturday morning.

But Danny could not wait. "Peachy!" he hissed to his friend. "Rise and shine! I've got to tell you something."

Peachy just rolled over and grunted, mumbling a few indistinct words.

"Peachy, wake up," Danny insisted. He shook Peachy by the shoulder. Peachy jumped, gasping as though he had seen a ghost.

"Oy, Danny," Peachy complained, rubbing his eyes. "Are you daft? What do you want with me this early?"

"Peachy, listen! This is important. Do you remember telling me that you hated it when we do all the work and Mr. Holmes solves the case?"

"Yeah? What of it?"

Danny looked triumphant. "This time it's all up to us. Mr. Holmes isn't even on the right track. The snake-bite didn't kill the man . . . don't you see? That's the clue if we can just figure out what it means. Get dressed! We need to go see the coroner who got it wrong."

"When? Now?"

"Right after chapel."

———

Chapel was an every-morning occurrence at Waterloo Road. Lord Shaftesbury, who founded the school, believed that young people needed to be well cared for, loved, and educated, but that was not all. He knew that they needed to understand that God cared for them, too, and that seeking his guidance was the only route to a successful life.

As a result, the school had prayer and Bible study every day and a speaker on Saturday. This particular weekend it was Headmaster Ingram's turn to address the students.

Danny found his attention wandering from the message. He caught himself several times making a mental list of questions to ask and answers to seek, just like Sherlock Holmes would do.

Then something Master Ingram said caught Danny's attention. The head of the school used the word "poison." *What an odd coincidence,* Danny thought. Then the coincidence was repeated.

"Sin is just like a deadly poison," Master Ingram said again. "It harms us all. You cannot live in this world and escape it. Once it's in your life, your spirit will surely die, unless you obtain the antidote. And do you know what that is?"

Danny was all attention now, and he could see that Peachy, sleepy as he was, had perked up also.

The headmaster continued, "The blood of Jesus is the only remedy for the poison of sin. And the good news is, the cure never fails. No matter how wicked the sin or how deadly the fault, the blood of Jesus, applied to your heart, will never fail to save, cure, and heal."

Danny looked at Peachy and raised his eyebrows. Maybe this message was a sign that they were on the right track . . . and maybe it was a warning as well. When it was time for the closing prayer, Danny sincerely asked for help from the Lord.

———

It was a long walk through the streets of London to St. Bartholomew's Hospital. Known familiarly to Londoners as Bart's, the medical buildings were located clear across the river from the school and all the way east by Smithfield Market.

The boys arrived outside the west gate, just below a statue of King Henry the Eighth. No one was moving about the grounds. *Good,* Danny thought, *this will give us an opportunity to do our work without being bothered.*

They walked through the front doors of the hospital and stopped at a large, oak desk. Danny assumed that there was supposed to be someone on duty, but no one was present. "Peachy," Danny said, "who did the paper say was in charge of the examination of the dead man?"

"Some Malky or Monkey . . . something I can't remember."

Duff smiled and laughed. "Monkey!" he repeated.

Peachy chuckled at his own joke while Danny read a sign posted by the desk that listed the doctors' names under various departments within the hospital.

"Aha!" he exclaimed, sounding very much like Sherlock Holmes pouncing on a clue. "Here it is. Malpied in patholo-gy."

"That's pathology," Peachy teased. "C'mon now, Danny. We learned that word in class a long time ago."

Danny ignored him and looked on a map for the doctor's office location. "Downstairs," he said, then added softly, "next to the morgue."

The basement level of the building was even quieter than the lobby. The gas lamps were turned low, and not a single footstep could be heard.

Peachy noticed the thick, pungent odor that lingered in the air. He nudged Danny. "Hey, Danny. You smell something?"

Danny nodded somberly. "It's what they use to preserve dead bodies," he said.

Duff stopped cold when he heard that. "No, no, no, no . . ." he repeated to himself.

"It's all right, Duff," Danny said. "We won't see any."

A short distance down the hall they came to a sign that read:

PATHOLOGY
Ryan Malpied, M.D.
CHIEF OF SERVICE

Peachy tried the door, rattling the latch. It was locked, but he noticed a thin ribbon of light under the door.

"Who's there?" a voice called out. The door swung open, and they saw a short man in a white lab coat. "What do you want?" he demanded. The man looked at the group from behind his spectacles, squinting up at Duff in the poor light.

Danny swallowed hard. "We've come to see Dr. Malpied."

"Aye, that's me." Malpied dropped his gaze, and Danny could see his features. He was a stocky man with a sharp face. He looked kind but overworked; his eyes had dark circles below them. Danny could hear his Scottish accent plainly. "What would ye have, then?"

"Sir," Peachy stepped forward, taking charge of the conversation, "we've come about the man who died two days ago during the Persian Society dinner for the Peacock Crown."

"Aye," Malpied said. "I know the case. What's your business?"

"Well, sir," Peachy continued, "you said he died of a snakebite."

"Aye, that I did. Are ye questioning my diagnosis?"

"We saw the snake, sir, and it has no bite."

"You're no making sense, laddie."

Danny cut in to explain. "What he means to say, sir, is that the snake that bit the man had no venom sacks. We saw the snake at the zoological grounds. The reptile keeper confirmed that the snake has no poison."

"How can that be true? It was clearly heart failure

brought on by the poison. Classic case. How can you children . . . why, I don't even know who ye are!"

"Beg pardon again, sir," Danny said. "The reptile keeper explained the dying symptoms, and it's just not as fast as all that. I understand it's hard to believe, but we have the man's name at the zoo, Rajeev Goa. You can ask him yourself."

Malpied thought for a few moments. "Who are ye anyway, and what's this aboot, then?"

"We," Danny paused for dramatic effect, "are the Baker Street Brigade. We work for Sherlock Holmes."

The doctor looked impressed but still doubtful. "I suppose I could ask Mr. Holmes also?"

"Not exactly," Peachy said. "Holmes doesn't know of this bit of news just yet." Dr. Malpied eyed him suspiciously. "That's not to say that he won't . . . in fact, we're going there right now. Right, Danny?" Peachy stammered.

Danny nodded.

"Ye go there then," Malpied said. "I'll examine the body again and join ye there. If I arrive at Baker Street and don't find ye . . ." He thought about his next words. "I suppose it won't matter if ye come or no, I'll probably never see ye again."

Danny looked the doctor squarely in the face. "We'll be there."

———

Sherlock Holmes listened intently to the report of the boys, whom Holmes called his Baker Street Irregulars, as they waited in Holmes's study for Dr. Malpied to arrive. The famous detective sat in the chair that had been recovered from the top of the police van. The study was clear of smoke, but there was a lingering film of oily black soot on several of the unbroken windows. When Mrs. Hudson, the housekeeper, returned from her trip, she would surely have a fit. Peachy thought he would enjoy seeing Mr. Holmes reprimanded, if only there were a safe place from which to watch the scene.

The investigator smoked a long church warden pipe, filling the room with the pungent aroma of Turkish tobacco. He smiled and chuckled to himself as he reviewed the news about the snake.

Danny and Peachy waited patiently on a sofa across from Holmes, fascinated by the workings of his mind. Duff looked out the broken window at the passing carriages. Sensing that silence was necessary at this meeting, he imitated his friends and remained quiet.

Holmes blurted out suddenly, "If this is true, then the murder case against the Guardian cult member falls apart. Of course there is still the attempted theft of the crown." Holmes explained how Clair Avery, unable to locate the boys earlier in the day, had come to him with the news about the burglar's capture. Then the sleuth continued, "If mysterious happenings continue . . ." He paused and gave a hollow laugh that sent a chill up Danny's spine. "One thing you can be sure of, gentlemen, there is more to this curse than you know."

Danny saw Peachy turn pale and knew his friend was remembering their experience in the museum cellar. Danny stared at the woven Oriental rug and tried to imagine what Holmes was thinking. "What do you mean by the curse, Mr. Holmes? I thought you said before that you had this case all wrapped up."

"Well, Wiggins, it would appear that there is more to this matter than I could first imagine. All of it will be uncovered in due time. Meanwhile, however, be careful. I wouldn't want my Irregulars damaged in any way. You've proven to be very valuable to me and my work. In fact, I would not be involved with this case had you not brought this evidence to my attention."

Just then there was a knock at the door. "Ah, that will be our Dr. Malpied now. I'm very interested to hear what his findings are." Peachy was already heading downstairs to admit the coroner.

Danny reviewed their conclusions while Malpied ascended the stairs. *What if we're wrong?* he wondered.

Holmes rose as Peachy reentered the sitting room with Dr. Malpied following close behind him. "Ah, Dr. Malpied, I presume." Holmes extended a hand, but Malpied did not take it. The doctor was pale, and his fingers trembled as he held his hat in his hand.

"Mr. 'Olmes," Malpied began, "I am a very confused man. As your assistants suggested, there were no traces of venom in the victim's blood. Just now I was able to identify the cause of death as a heart attack." He paused and rubbed his forehead. His voice shook as he continued. "But Mr. 'Olmes, there was no reason for this man to die; his heart was healthy. He must have been scared to death."

Holmes, who had returned to his seat, puffed his pipe before answering. "Most peculiar indeed."

SIX

THE SEVEN DIALS District of central London was notorious for the high number of pickpockets and thugs, otherwise known as buzzers and rampsmen. The area was named for the seven sundials placed in a ring where seven streets converged. The center of the circle boasted a large stone column. It was at this easily remembered spot that the lawless of all professions met.

Seven Dials was also where Sherlock Holmes knew he could find his informant, Nathan DuBois. Besides being a nose, DuBois translated stolen goods and fingered likely victims for robbery. But his greatest trade was in news. Holmes merely had to pay DuBois a small sum of money to start him talking about any subject that might concern the criminal world. Holmes had often considered turning in DuBois for his petty crimes, but he did not. The sleuth realized that DuBois was valuable for the information he provided about the larger schemes of the London underworld.

Peachy, Danny, and Duff approached the scene first.

The boys were dressed in their toughest clothes, cloth caps pulled low over their foreheads. Leaving Danny and Duff as lookouts, Peachy advanced into the square.

Walking toward the central column, Peachy darted his eyes back and forth to see who was watching. All around he could see the crime birds of the rookery. One man, cleaning his nails with the point of a rusty knife, glared as he walked past. It was a dangerous place to be, especially with dark coming soon, but Holmes did not want to risk being spotted here by anyone who might recognize him.

Peachy spoke to a short man with shifty eyes who leaned against the column. "Are you the one they call DeMoney?" he asked.

The man looked at Peachy and spat a large puddle of tobacco juice at his feet. "Maybe I is," he said, "and maybe I ain't. 'Oo wants to know?"

"I have a message," Peachy replied, "from a buyer named S." DuBois smiled, showing a gap of several missing teeth in the top row.

"S. says," Peachy began, "that he's interested in buying a Persian rug. And he wants to know where he can find one. But he also . . ."

"Did 'e send the money wif you?" DuBois interrupted. "Do you 'ave it on you?" He began grabbing at Peachy, patting him down in search of coins. "Listen, chavvy, I could burk you and no one the wiser . . " DuBois cut himself short when another man walked up behind Peachy and grabbed the boy's shoulder.

The second man spoke harshly. "What 'ave we 'ere?" The newcomer laughed. "A little babe 'oo's lost?"

Peachy did not move. Across the courtyard, Danny and Duff watched. Danny smiled.

"'Ere now." DuBois grabbed the man's hand, removing it from Peachy's shoulder. "You leave this lad to me." The other man clearly did not like being touched. He seized DuBois's arm and twisted it around behind his back.

Peachy ran back to rejoin his friends. DuBois gasped in pain as the taller fellow forced his hand higher between his shoulder blades. "Take care, DuBois," the wiry stranger warned. DuBois shuddered when he recognized the voice of Sherlock Holmes. "If you ever harm my assistants, I will personally arrange that you never see daylight again."

"Why, Mr. 'Olmes!" DuBois whined. "I'd never 'urt the little nipper, I swear!"

"See that you don't!" the detective advised. "And now you will tell me what I wish to know." Holmes released DuBois's arm.

Cleverly concealed behind a street thug's appearance, Holmes sported muttonchop whiskers, a bulb-shaped nose, and a somehow-missing ear—all part of the amazing costume. The detective's clothes were dirty, his shoes holey and worn. Holmes smiled when he saw the look on DuBois's face, but he slapped the informant's hand away when he reached up to touch the fake nose.

"Just tell me what I asked," Holmes demanded.

"I'm not sure I know what you mean, Mr. 'Olmes," DuBois lied, obviously hoping for some money.

Holmes became irritated. "Listen, DuBois, you have a history of petty crimes that would impress the magistrates. Or I might just tell Willie the Arm how you fingered him in that bank job. Now, I suggest you tell me what I wish to know for free this time, as I am in a foul mood."

The children could hear Holmes elevate his voice in anger and laughed as DuBois cringed. Other people around the circle were beginning to notice also.

"Quiet down, Mr. 'Olmes," DuBois begged. "In Rose Street, just across from Tipman's Jewelers, there is a pub called the Lamb and Flag. For a bit o' silver you can be admitted into the cellar. Underneaf the pub is a gambling hall. I fink you can find what you're after there."

"Very well. I thank you." Holmes walked toward the Brigade, and they all went on together, heading south out of the circle.

———

Duff watched through the window of the pub and reported to Danny and Peachy on Holmes's progress. Still in disguise, Holmes strutted to the large, cherry wood bar, signaling the bartender for service. Peachy listened to Duff's narration while Danny looked for another way into the basement. When the hulking barkeep came to Holmes, Duff could see them speaking. Holmes laid down a five-pound note.

The barman motioned for Holmes to follow him around to the end of the countertop. There he pointed to a staircase sunken in the floor, leading down to the basement. Holmes nodded and descended.

"Mr. Holmes is gone," Duff concluded.

"Good then," Danny said. "We can find our own way in now."

Peachy shook his head. "I'm not so sure that's a good idea, Danny. What if there's trouble?"

"All the more reason for us to be there for Mr. Holmes. Now c'mon, I've spotted another door." Peachy and Duff followed Danny a short way up the street where they came to a small alley, barely big enough to walk through. In the darkness, Duff stumbled over a pile of trash and bumped Peachy.

"Watch it, mate," Peachy complained. "I've only got two feet, and if you break one . . ."

"Sssh!" Danny scolded. "Here we are," he said as he knelt over a large wooden square in the concrete. Danny brushed away years of dirt from an iron ring that served as the trapdoor handle.

Peachy looked at Danny as though he were crazy. "Crikey! This is no door. You've gone bloomin' glocky." Danny ignored him and tugged on the ring.

"I can do it," Duff said and stepped in front of Danny to lift the trapdoor easily from its resting place. Instantly they could hear loud music, laughter, and shouting coming from the basement.

Danny lay on the ground and peered into the darkness below. As his eyes adjusted he could see wine kegs and the shape of a door outlined by light and noise around its edges.

"I'm going in," Danny said. "Peachy, you stay here with . . ."

"Oh, no! No, sir, I'm coming in with you." Peachy crossed his arms to show that he would not be argued with. Danny shrugged and lowered himself down the opening.

"There's no ladder," Danny said. "Duff, you need to stay up here to help us out when we leave."

Peachy spoke to Duff as Danny dropped down the hole. "You hear that, Duffer? You stay here and give us a hand when we call for you." Duff nodded, but with a blank look on his face. Peachy thought how easily this excursion could go wrong. "Just stay here," he repeated forcefully.

As Peachy lowered his legs through the opening, he felt a hand grasp his ankle. "Oh thanks, Dan . . ."

The red-haired boy was unable to finish his sentence before the hand snapped him downward, making him lose his grip and hit his chin on the ledge. Peachy scrambled away on the cellar floor. A figure loomed above him in the pale light that shone through the trapdoor.

The crumpled, silent form of Danny lay on the floor across the room from him. Peachy heard Duff calling from the alley, "Daa-nny, Pea-chy. I don't like this here."

Peachy rolled his eyes and felt the lump on his chin. His captor reached for Peachy's collar and pulled the boy up to his knees. "Tell your mate to lower himself in 'ere, or I'll cut your throat."

The man's breath was foul. Peachy's assailant struck him on the head with the handle of a knife to show he was serious. The Baker Street Irregular fell back to the floor.

"It gets worse," the menacing figure hissed. "Call your mate."

Peachy felt a warm trickle of blood run down his face, and he obeyed the instruction. "Duff, come down. Bring yourself down here." In a moment Peachy could see Duff's feet dangling over the edge of the trapdoor.

Duff hopped down effortlessly and stood in the center of the room, waiting for his eyes to adjust to the darkness. "Cor, you're a big fella," the captor said. "Sit down." Duff did not follow the order fast enough and was struck. He did not fall as Peachy had done, but cried out, unsure of why he had been hit.

From the shadows, a revived Danny charged the man, knocking him to the floor. The knife flew off into the corner of the room. Peachy jumped on top of the man and pummeled the back of his neck and head.

Danny grabbed their captor around the knees and yelled for Duff to help. Duff sat still and sniffled, confused by the commotion. The sinister bloke found the strength to stand with Peachy on his back and Danny clinging to his legs.

Peachy squeezed tight around the man's neck, trying to choke him. It was not working.

"Help, Duff!" Danny yelled again.

Duff ran forward, still confused. "Is that you, Danny?"

"Too right it's me," Danny panted. "Help!"

"What do I do?"

Just then the man turned around and growled fiercely in Duff's face. The sudden animal sound caused the large boy to react without thinking. A single blow was quickly delivered from Duff's massive fist, making the man fall to his knees. The thug's eyes rolled back and he slumped over.

Danny stood up and patted Duff on the back. "Good job, Duffer! You saved our . . ."

"Can you save the congrats?" Peachy wheezed. "Give us a hand here," he called from the floor. His arms were still locked around the man's neck. The combination of his own weight and the man's bulk kept them pinned underneath the unconscious assailant.

Danny grabbed the man's shoulder and heaved him up, freeing Peachy. Next Danny found a lantern and a box of matches under a table. Lighting the wick, the leader of the Brigade saw that they were in a small storeroom with one door. The space was filled with kegs and chairs and various supplies for the bar upstairs. Danny also noticed, with some amusement, that all four of the room's occupants had bloody noses and split lips. They could not have been more banged up if they had been in an all-day, schoolyard brawl.

When Danny shared this observation, Peachy replied, "Why is that funny? I hurt."

"We're alive," Duff observed, wiping his bleeding nose on his sleeve.

The unknown attacker began to stir. Danny quickly scanned the room for some rope and tied the figure securely to a large keg labeled "Strongbow Cider."

"Yes," Danny agreed, pulling the knots tight. "We are alive. I hope we can say the same for Mr. Holmes. These are tough blokes."

"That reminds me," Peachy said, "what was this rotter doing down here in the dark?"

Danny looked around. "He came at me from that direction," he said, pointing to the northern wall. There were traces of fresh dirt under the table where he had found the lantern. Danny got down on his hands and knees and crawled under the table. "Look here, this chap's been busy." Danny began pulling loose bricks away from the wall and setting them aside.

Peachy joined Danny on the floor and saw the gaping hole in the wall. "It's a tunnel, Danny!" Peachy exclaimed, peering inside. "Here, Duff! Bring us that lantern." With the extra light they could see that the tunnel went at least thirty feet straight ahead before beginning a gradual turn to the left. It was shored up in several spots along the length and had iron candleholders spiked into every other post.

"Where do you suppose this leads?" Danny mused.

Peachy already knew the answer. "To the jewelry store," he said. "I wager it goes under the street to that Tipman's Jewelers."

"I bet you're right," Danny concurred.

"Oy!" A man's voice shouted from inside the tunnel. "What's on, then?"

Danny gasped and quickly blew out the lantern.

"We've got to get out!" Peachy whispered. They hurried to where Duff stood under the trapdoor. "Lift me up, Duff!" Peachy instructed.

Duff locked his hands and heaved Peachy through the square opening. Danny was stepping into Duff's hand when the door to the cellar suddenly swung open. It bumped the still unconscious man where he remained tied to the keg. Danny froze. A tall form stumbled into the room as though he had been pushed.

"That'll teach you to come nosin' around," someone in the cellar said as the new arrival crashed into the back wall. "You stay there 'til we decide what to do with you!" The door slammed shut again, and Danny could hear the lock click. The new captive slid down to rest on the floor. Danny and Duff stood perfectly still.

"Oy! Wake up!" came an impatient yell from the tunnel.

Then Peachy leaned over the trapdoor and said, "Crikey, Danny! Come on!"

Suddenly Danny panicked. "Duff! Up!" he shouted. Duff heaved with all his might, thrusting Danny to safety above. Duff raised his arms above his head, but it was too late. The newcomer to the cellar prison had grabbed Duff's shoulder. Duff turned and swung hard, hitting the man in the gut.

"Bernard," a familiar tone gasped, "it's me! Sherlock Holmes."

Danny heard the detective's voice and called down to him, "Mr. Holmes, come on! You don't have any time!"

Holmes helped Duff up and was being pulled up himself when a figure emerged from the tunnel with a lantern.

The thug tied to the keg awoke shaking his head. He spotted Holmes and Duff and cried out, "Thomas! Stop them!" At that moment Duff and Danny lost their grip on Sherlock, and he fell back to the floor.

Thomas, the one who had just emerged from the tunnel, punched Holmes squarely in the jaw, knocking the detective backward.

Peachy could see the man with the lantern directly below the trapdoor opening. He decided to take action. He gave Duff a mighty shove from behind. Duff flailed his arms, trying to regain his balance, but Peachy pushed him again and the large boy fell through the opening, crushing Thomas into silence.

Leaving one figure gagged and tied to the barrel and

Thomas knocked out on the cellar floor, the Baker Street Brigade hurried to make an exit before anyone else arrived.

"I've learned enough," Holmes said. "I now know the likely whereabouts of the Guardians."

"That's dandy," Peachy said. "Because I've had more than enough of this caper."

SEVEN

THERE WAS SELDOM a quiet spot along the Victoria Embankment that bound the north shore of the Thames River. So many people came out to walk along its banks and enjoy the breeze under the plane trees that there was a constant hum of conversation and laughter. On the streets that followed the shoreline there were innumerable carts and cabs, all making their own particular noises as they bounced along the cobblestones.

Peachy broke into a yell: "Extra, read all about it. Curse-ed Crown Causes Calamity." He walked away from Duff with an extra stack of the *London Times*.

The Irregulars always sold their daily allotment of papers in the following manner: Duff stood at a central location, holding all their stock. Danny and Peachy would come and get resupplied from him. The two friends also sold Duff's share, insuring that no one would take advantage of him.

Peachy walked up Buckingham Street a way, calling out several different headlines. Sometimes he rhymed the words or tried to find a phrase where all the words started with the same letter. This time it was hard to get variety. All the front page headlines had to do with the Peacock Crown. Either the columns announced the crown's next exhibition at the Royal Academy or commented on rumors of the curse or discussed the victim of the mysterious heart attack.

The subject of the crown was on everyone's lips, and no one was without a paper this day. Peachy's pile of the *Times* went fast, and he was constantly returning to Duff for more. Danny, who did not announce the headlines quite as loudly or poetically as Peachy, had the same results anyway. Soon all the papers were sold, and the work was done.

Danny returned to Duff's "standing spot." "That's it," Danny announced. "I've never sold so fast in my life. This crown and curse business has really got people talking."

Duff smiled but did not speak. Danny looked at him with a raised eyebrow, inviting Duff to comment, then shook his head. "C'mon, Duff," he said, taking his friend by the arm. "Let's go find Peachy."

Peachy was just up on the Strand, and he only had one paper left in his hand when they approached. "Well done," he said. "I was just about to come find you."

"Hurry up and sell that last one so we can go."

"No, I think I'll keep this one so I can read the inside too."

Danny looked astounded. "Haven't you had enough of this old news?"

Peachy shook his head. "There's more of this story on page four. It says . . ." Peachy cleared his throat and turned the pages. He began sounding out the words. "To-day will see . . . a press con . . . fer . . . ence. Today will see a press conference regarding the infamous Jew-elled Peacock of Persia. Mr. Douglas Macintire, the crown's im . . . pre . . . sario, will answer questions about the so-called curse."

"What's an im-pre-sario?" Duff wanted to know.

"A promoter, uhh, a booster. He's like a peddler, only he sells people the idea of wanting to see something, instead of selling them a thing to take home. Got it?"

Duff nodded wisely with a complete lack of compre-hension in his eyes.

Peachy shrugged and resumed, "You see, Danny? I always thought people just talked about the problem. Looks like this Macintire is going to try to do something about it."

"That's nice, but we can't get into that press confer-ence."

"I know that, but it's interesting to hear about it all."

"Amazing!" Danny mocked. "C'mon, let's go back to Trafalgar Square. Won't Cap'n Mewsley be impressed that we're already finished?"

———

Upon entering Trafalgar Square, Danny immediately located Mewsley, the paperboys' foreman. He was sitting near a large water fountain, beneath the shadow of Nel-son's Column. The large flat cart with metal wheels used for distributing all the papers to the newsies throughout the day sat next to him. The cart was empty now. In Mewsley's hand was one of his famous cheroots, an In-dian cigar, which stained his hands a pale yellow. His grizzled face split into a toothless grin as the group approached.

"Danny, my boy," remarked Mewsley, squinting up. "Finished already?"

Danny nodded and smiled. "The public is fascinated with the crown, Cap'n Mewsley. Not a single paper went unsold when Peachy barked his poetic headlines."

"Except one," Peachy reminded him. "I kept one to read for myself. I suppose I am as interested as anyone else."

"And Headmaster Ingram says it's good to read for practice," Duff observed. "I know the alphabet. Forward and backward."

Mewsley patted him on the back. "That's good, Duff, my lad. Why, you'll be head of this old newspaper in no time, dressin' in top hat and tails and ridin' in a carriage like the earl. Now hand me your spoils, gents, and I'll be fair with you."

Danny and Peachy emptied their pockets and delivered the coins to their foreman. When Mewsley totalled it all, he deducted their commission, divided it into three portions, and handed it back. "Congratulations, boys," he praised. "This makes a new record for you when you figger pay to hours worked. Very nice indeed. It reminds me of the time in Istanbul. Seems the sultan wanted to fortify the harem where he kept his four-and-twenty wives, and the major volunteered me and my company to help reinforce the walls. Turns out the walls were six feet thick already. Well, my commander told them they needed no thicker one than that, but the vizier insisted on paying us all anyways, for doin' nothing' . . . ah, those were grand days. Just after that . . ."

"Well, sir," Peachy interrupted, "we must be going. There's a meeting being held at the British Museum about the curse. And then we're off to the Royal Academy show."

"Hold on there, lad. Are you speaking of the Peacock Crown show for the big artistes?" Peachy nodded. "That meeting is closed to the public. You'll just have to read about it in print." Mewsley puffed on his little cigar.

"Yes, sir," Peachy said. "I know. But I bet we can get in somehow. If anything's going to happen, we're not going to miss it."

————

A crowd had begun to collect outside the British Museum. Three hundred onlookers already stood in the blazing heat.

In a few moments the press conference would begin, and with the huge turnout of spectators, archaeologist Patrick Gannon was growing nervous about security.

Gannon found Dreyer, the curator, standing by a podium just inside the entrance. "Dreyer," Gannon spoke in an authoritative whisper, "may I have a word?"

"Quite," Dreyer replied, walking with him into a curtained alcove. "What is the matter?"

Gannon rubbed his neck and tilted his head back to study the ceiling. Looking back at Dreyer he said, "I'm concerned about this Royal Academy show . . . protection for the crown . . . that sort of thing."

"You need not worry, Mr. Gannon," Dreyer reassured the crown's discoverer. "Mr. Macintire has made extremely thorough arrangements, including guards at every exit and additional guards on the second floor."

"Lestrade and others of his level of professionalism?" Gannon commented sarcastically.

"No, no," Dreyer chuckled at the dry wit. "Actually it's a private security team, highly qualified and well trained for this sort of thing."

Gannon sighed. "I'm sure Macintire's done a good job, but I think there should be a search team at the front door."

"Dear me! Searching for what?" Dreyer asked incredulously.

"Weapons, reptiles . . . I don't know . . . anything suspicious."

Douglas Macintire was walking past the screened recess and overheard the conversation. He flung back the curtain with a smirk. "I don't think we can keep notable personalities waiting in the heat while we feel everyone's pockets," he growled.

"Maybe that is a bit extreme, but . . ." Gannon hesitated.

"But what?" Macintire interrupted irritably. "I'm promoting this exhibition, and I've got security under control. We're not spending extra dollars . . . my dollars! . . . on something that is unnecessary. We're most definitely not going to scare off any visitors who already might be frightened enough by the curse nonsense to turn away as it is." He raised his eyebrows at Gannon. "Are you clear on my position?" he demanded. Then without waiting for a reply, he stalked off.

"I'm not in favor of scaring anyone away," Dreyer whined after the promoter, just to show whose side he was on.

On the financial side Macintire was correct, Gannon

mused. A quarter of the money made from the upcoming museum exhibition would belong to him. Security was not the archaeologist's responsibility, and lower costs meant more shillings in his own pocket. Why should he worry about it?

"I'm sorry," Dreyer said, shrugging his shoulders. "That's just the way it is."

"No, that's quite all right," Gannon responded with his hands raised and his head cocked to the side. "Thanks."

The small platform erected in front of the steps of the British Museum was surrounded by newspaper reporters shouting questions at Douglas Macintire. The promoter waited patiently by the podium for order to sweep over the crowd. His air was that of an impatient schoolteacher waiting for his class to quiet down before he allowed them to hear his important lecture.

"Gentlemen," he finally began, "I have just a few comments before I take your questions one at a time. First of all, I realize the tragedy of the last few days' events. It is a terrible thing indeed that someone died. I can guarantee that nothing supernatural or ghostly is involved with the appearance of the snake in the museum. There is no curse."

Macintire was not allowed to continue his statement. The crowd of reporters erupted again, provoked by his outrageously casual comments. Again he waited for quiet before resuming.

"As I was saying, the strange occurrence has nothing to do with long-dead Persian kings or any so-called hex. I want to stress the fact that there is no curse. The Peacock Crown of ancient Persia is an artifact of rare and wondrous beauty but nothing more! I repeat, the rumors of an evil spell attached to the crown are ridiculous and have no place in our modern society where everything can be explained with science."

"How do you explain the disaster then?" Robinson of the *Daily Standard* managed to shout before Macintire continued.

"I have no explanation. It is not scientific to venture an explanation without sufficient study. At this time it appears scientific knowledge is limited in this regard. Please, I ask you, do not speculate idly in print; do not spin rumors into widespread belief by printing them in your papers. Please, gentlemen, show a little restraint!"

The horde of reporters quickly scribbled those comments into their notebooks. Pierson of the *Mail* wrote "Promoter cannot explain away curse." Burbidge, reporting for the *Tribune,* wrote "Macintire says mysterious deadly snake is not part of an evil spell." Already every reporter in the crowd was making plans to do exactly the opposite of what Macintire had asked: They would make the curse the headline of tomorrow's account. Everyone knew that the phrase "curse may strike again" would fill the lungs of newsies and be on the lips of every citizen of London and beyond.

"Now I will take your questions."

Simpson, a writer for the *London Times,* stepped forward. "Mr. Macintire, aren't you worried that a strange event might occur again, leading to more innocent deaths?"

"Sir, I'm sure you are intelligent enough to realize

that we will tighten security to the point that nothing like that is possible," Macintire responded brusquely. "Special guards will be placed around the perimeter just in case, and everyone who comes to the exhibition will undergo a thorough scrutiny. After the Royal Academy show, we are expecting the largest crowd ever to attend the public display. The staff of the British Museum and I are prepared for any eventuality. Yes, you there." Macintire pointed to another reporter in the front of the pack who had patiently raised his hand and waited.

"There is talk that you will be held responsible should another accident occur. Aren't you at all worried?"

"No, sir, I am not. Next? Yes?"

"It is said that the religious faction called the Guardians might be responsible for those events. How do you respond to that?"

"Gentlemen, I have seen no mysterious Persian figures lurking about, and certainly none could get past my guards. Now, if you'll excuse me, I have preparations to attend to for the show. This interview is at an end."

The crowd roared and lunged forward, screaming their last queries at him: "Is it true there is a Persian in custody? Was there a robbery attempt? Did you and Mr. Gannon argue about security measures?"

Macintire shoved past them all, saying, "No comment." The American promoter fled to the safety of his office inside the museum.

EIGHT

JUST EAST OF Old Bond Street and north of Piccadilly were the buildings of the Royal Academy of Arts. It was the headquarters and gallery of the most respected group of artists in England. The five-story structure, with its sweeping spiral staircase, displayed treasures of the art world by Michelangelo, da Vinci, and others.

On the topmost floor was an exhibition hall with immensely high ceilings. In midsummer it usually offered a showing of the most recent work by the academy's members, but this year those paintings had been cleared out and stored. The academy had been invited to draw, sketch, and paint the fabulous jewelled crown. The artists and their guests would number close to five hundred people. Many had brought their families to what was already being called the chance to see "the infamous Persian Peacock."

There were so many children attending the Royal Academy show that the Baker Street Brigade got into the building easily. "If we split up," Danny said, "we can look around much faster." So it was agreed in the foyer at the bottom of the spiral stairs that Danny and Clair would stay on the exhibit floor and watch the proceedings while Duff and Peachy would search for anything suspicious.

Peachy and Duff walked back across the marble-tiled lobby to snoop around. Danny led Clair up to the top floor. Inside, people milled around looking at the array of Persian artifacts prepared by Macintire and Gannon to set the mood for the crown. Macintire had realized that the peacock alone would be dwarfed by the crowd. The other pieces ranged from large stone figures with strange bearded faces to simple children's toys that were a thousand years old.

Danny walked past the displays with little interest, while Clair stopped to examine each one. When Danny noticed she had stopped, he turned back and tried to look attentive. "These are . . . fascinating," he said, wanting Clair to think that he was refined and gentlemanly. Danny knew that Peachy was competing for her interest and that he had to try extra hard to win it.

"Aren't they?" she replied. "My mother went to Persia. She got back just before she passed away. Some doctors thought it might have been an illness that she contracted while she was there. But our family physician knew it was tuberculosis from the beginning."

"I'm sorry," Danny said. It pained him to know that anyone else had lost a parent. He could understand the way Clair felt every time she thought of her mother. He missed his also.

"I would like to go there someday," Clair said. "I hear it is a place of mystery and excitement. Mother told me all about it when she came home. I sat next to her bed in the hospital and listened to the stories for days. Then one day the doctor would not let me in to see her. I was not surprised. She coughed all the time and couldn't breathe well enough to finish one sentence. But . . ." the girl paused, staring at the clay fragments of a small, angel-like figurine in a glass case. "I could've seen her, Danny. I wouldn't have cried. I could've seen her."

"I know. I understand. I wish I could have seen my parents too. It'll get better. It just takes time. It'll get easier," he said gently. Clair didn't cry, and Danny admired her for that.

They continued walking along the row of artifacts on display. However, Danny was looking for other things— for danger, for suspicious behavior, and for clues to the mystery.

———

Peachy and Duff went all the way up the spiral stairs to the landing above the exhibit. When Peachy discovered a small wooden panel set in the wall, he and Duff climbed into it unseen. They found that they were in the attic directly over the crowd. There were even ventilation holes in the ceiling through which they could observe the throng below. "That cheat," Peachy mumbled to himself as he spied Danny, strolling hand-in-hand with Clair.

The ornately swirled plaster ceiling of the exhibition gallery was hung by wires from the rafters above. Peachy and Duff were in the space between the false ceiling and the real beams.

In the center of the attic was a catwalk also suspended from the timbers above. Peachy realized that someone who stepped off the narrow walkway might plunge through the plaster and fall thirty feet to the floor below.

On both sides of the wooden walk were cables that travelled down through small openings in strange trapdoors. Peachy saw that the ropes suspended the chandeliers lighting the room beneath. The trapdoors allowed workmen to raise and clean the light fixtures.

Peachy lay down next to a chandelier's hinged panel with his legs still resting on the catwalk and his body projecting over the ceiling. He gazed down through the cable opening, frustrated at being stuck so far away from Clair.

"What?" Duff asked. "Are you sick, or did you see something get stoled?"

"Oh, nothing, Duff. Listen, it's hard to see up here. Let's walk down to the far end and then leave."

"Yes, it's hard to see and scary things go in places like that," Duff commented.

Peachy laughed a little, and they continued to the end of the creaky catwalk. "Now I know why there's no light up here," he explained. "There's nothing to see." He bent down again and looked through another chandelier hole. Grinning wickedly, he picked up a pinch of the crumbling plaster of which the ceiling was made. Closing one eye, Peachy aimed for the head of his comrade below and released the pebbly mixture. It tinkled through the crystals in the chandelier and fell, just missing Danny's hair. "Too bad." Peachy shrugged. "I . . ."

All at once there was a commotion below. The

crowd screamed and crowded toward the only staircase. Unthinking, Peachy crawled off the boards to get a better view through a ventilation grate. From his new location he could see the stampeding mob. People were shouting, "The curse! The curse!"

Behind the horde was a heap of snakes slithering across the tile floor like a tangled pile of ropes. They seemed to have come out of thin air. Even the serpents themselves seemed panicked, Peachy noticed. They mostly turned away from the screaming mass of people and found refuge under glass cabinets.

Peachy was so enthralled with the action that he did not notice the ceiling beginning to give way under his weight. It creaked and moaned, sounding a warning, but the commotion below was louder. Then the plaster burst and Peachy fell headfirst. He clutched for a chandelier cable and caught it. Hanging at an odd angle with his feet on the brass support, he swung wildly above the crowd. Plaster and a trapdoor fell, narrowly missing a display case and splintering on the floor.

Duff leaned over the handrail of the walkway, staring down at Peachy in bewilderment. "Help me!" Peachy yelled.

Grabbing the cable and tugging hand over hand, Duff managed to pull Peachy back up to the level of the ceiling. Peachy freed one hand from the rope and made a grab for the edge of the walkway. He hoisted himself up as Duff continued to raise the chandelier. At last Peachy was safe.

The exhibition was in total chaos, and the little drama above had gone unnoticed.

Danny shielded Clair as the panicked crush of people swarmed toward them. The two backed into a corner between a case of ancient clay tablets and a headless stone statue on a granite pedestal. Clair made no sound as her terror grew unbearably. Danny caught sight of one of the snakes and grimaced, hoping it would not come their way.

As the hall quickly emptied, it became eerily quiet. Danny shivered when he realized that the only creatures left were Clair, himself, and the snakes. Cautiously he stepped forward, peeking right, then left, up the entire length of the gallery. He saw the tail ends of several snakes slide under displays, but none was close to where they stood. The worst of the alarm seemed over.

"Let's get out of here," he said, walking forward. "Let's get out before something else happens."

It was at that instant that Danny saw the fat, brown diamond shape of a viper's head poke around the corner of the statue's pedestal. It was only inches from Clair's feet.

Without thought in a sudden burst of action, Danny grabbed Clair around the waist and swung her up onto the pedestal beside the statue.

He felt a second of relief that Clair was safe—and then froze and bent over in pain. The muscles in his neck spasmed, and he grabbed his leg. The boy let out a chilling scream and collapsed to the floor. His reptile attacker hissed and slithered away to find shelter in another part of the room.

Danny moaned and his eyes rolled backward in his head. His face was very red, and Clair began to yell,

"Help! Help me!" She thought she heard Peachy's voice, but it was muffled and far away. She heard other voices as a door opened and closed. "Please help, he's been bitten!"

Douglas Macintire and Patrick Gannon appeared in front of her. "No!" Gannon shouted as he bent down to lift Danny up. The dark-haired boy vomited and went limp. Clair turned away and covered her eyes. Now she was crying.

Macintire touched her shoulder. "There, there," he said kindly. "I'm sure he'll be fine."

Clair faced the American with dread in her eyes. "How? Only one in one hundred can survive. How will he?"

———

Heat-weary London revived its perspiring activities the morning after Danny's injury. The street below his window in Bart's was crowded with sweat-drenched, puffing horses and sweat-drenched, cursing teamsters.

In some unreasonable way it angered Peachy to see people carrying on ordinary business while his friend Danny lay within inches of death. Peachy gazed down on Hosier Lane and the traffic going and coming from Smithfield Market. He tried to ignore the noise.

Peachy was caught between irritation at the outside world and wanting to forget the circumstances inside the hospital room. Danny tossed and turned, feverish and delirious. At times he would scream, and then he would lie still and shiver in the bed. But he never opened his eyes. When he moaned, it was so pitiful that Peachy wanted to cry.

I mustn't, Peachy thought. *Clair's here . . . Duff's watching me.* He squeezed his eyes tight, and a single teardrop fell on the dusty window ledge.

Faking a yawn, Peachy turned from the window and tried to pretend he was wiping sleep from his eyes. He looked around the white room, partitioned by a curtain. The doctors had long since removed the other patient, however, when Danny's agonized groans had been too disturbing. Peachy gritted his teeth at the thought.

Clair did not speak, but she looked up at Peachy from where she sat on the opposite side of Danny's bed. She held Danny's hand.

Duff looked confused, and his face was contorted into a mask of grief. All night he had not removed his gaze from Danny as the boy grew progressively worse. Twice the nurses had entered the room and tried to tell Duff to leave, but he did not respond. Even when they stood in front of him, blocking his view, he ignored them, merely leaning to the side to keep a careful, unending watch on his friend.

Peachy thought Duff was lucky not to understand how serious Danny's condition really was. He settled into a chair and tried to dismiss the unpleasant thought.

A doctor in a white laboratory jacket entered the room, stepping over Duff's legs and walking to the bedside. Placing a hand on Danny's forehead to keep him still, he placed a thermometer in Danny's mouth. "Good morning, children," he said. "I am Dr. Benson. I'm taking care of Danny."

Duff looked like a concerned hen brooding over a chick. He did not know this doctor, and he did not like the stranger touching his friend.

Benson looked at the thermometer and left the room shaking his head. Peachy stood and followed Benson out. "Doctor?" he asked. "How bad is he?"

"Much the same," the doctor said cautiously, putting his hand on Peachy's shoulder. "Listen, son, you three are just in the way. Why don't you all go home and rest?"

Peachy pulled away from him. "You're not doing anything at all! How can we be in the way if you're not helping?" He glanced up to see Clair watching through the curtain. Peachy slouched out of earshot and waited for the doctor to follow.

When Dr. Benson came out, Peachy repeated the question.

"Young man, we don't know how to cure him." Peachy swallowed hard. "But we're doing what we can. Please believe me, all of us are praying for your friend to recover."

"I'm sorry, sir. I suppose we . . ." At that moment Patrick Gannon appeared at the top of the staircase, and Peachy cut himself off. When Gannon saw the boy standing with the doctor, he walked toward them.

"Carnehan, is it?" Gannon asked. Benson turned from Peachy to face the archaeologist. "I've come to visit Danny," Gannon said. I brought a gift . . . some flowers."

"Why?" Peachy asked, the pain showing in every vibration of his frame. "He won't wake up to see them!" He began to cry, and his words were difficult to understand. "You and your stupid crown and your curse!"

"I . . . I'm sorry. I never meant for anything like this to happen. I never knew . . ."

"Well, it did happen! Danny's bit, and the reptile

man said only one in a hundred people could survive. What if Danny's not the one?" Dr. Benson put his arm around Peachy and drew him close. Peachy shook free of the embrace and stormed back into the room, leaving the two men of science in painful silence.

"I don't know what to say . . ." Gannon said awkwardly. "Doctor, what's being done for the boy?"

Benson spoke calmly, though he was shaken by Peachy's emotion. "We're waiting. We don't know how to cure him, but Mr. Holmes is working with his lab in Baker Street for a solution. The venom of the hearth viper is strange. It attacks the nervous system, causing brain damage if left unchecked. No one here has seen the like . . ."

"I know what I can do!" Gannon interrupted. "The library of the British Museum has an enormous amount of medical literature. Perhaps I could find something there."

Benson shrugged and commented on the unlikely odds, but Gannon was already striding away.

Peachy emerged again from the hospital room. A loud wail from Danny followed him. "Is it true, Dr. Benson? Is Holmes really working on a cure?"

"Yes, son, he's doing all he can, along with every poison specialist and tropical disease researcher on staff. If there's a cure . . ." Peachy was already heading out the door in Gannon's wake by the time Benson finished his thought.

NINE

WHEN PEACHY BURST through the door at Baker Street, he could hear the gurgling sounds of Holmes's laboratory in operation. The freckled boy ran up the stairs, hope for Danny's cure speeding him on. He reached the top, entered the sitting room, and found Holmes fast asleep on his sofa.

"Mr. Holmes!" Peachy shouted. "What are you doing?"

"Ah, Carnehan," Holmes yawned. "I'm merely catching up on some rest as I wait for my formula to crystallize."

Peachy smiled with relief. "You have one? An antidote to the poison? I thought it was impossible."

"Nothing is impossible, dear boy. It merely takes time. I needed a snake, a hearth viper, from which to extract venom. Lestrade had to fetch me one, and he brought me the wrong kind. It had to be returned. Then I had to milk the venom from the viper, boil the solution, and at present . . ."

"Never mind!" Peachy exclaimed. "Will it work?"

Holmes dropped his cheery manner, and in its place was serious regard. "I'm unsure at this time."

"When will you know? We're running out of time!"

"I will know when it is finished. Have patience. I have to test it on one of the mice first."

"Mice?" Peachy asked, looking around at a cage of squeaking rodents on the floor by the coal scuttle.

"Oh, Carnehan. It is made from venom, after all; we must proceed cautiously. What? Would you have me test it on Danny first?"

"Well, I . . ."

"No! Of course not! That would be very dangerous. Observe." Holmes lifted a half-full syringe labeled with a skull and crossbones. "This is a solution which I tried. It failed. It kills instantly. In fact, it's more potent than the snake's own toxin. Shall I demonstrate?" The detective stooped over the mice, who panicked and raced around their small enclosure.

Peachy cried out, "Don't! If you already know, don't kill another one."

"Exactly, Carnehan. Would you have our sick friend be the next mouse?"

Peachy shook his head. "But when will the cure be ready?"

"Technically, it's not a cure. The latest batch shows promise . . ."

"When?" Peachy demanded.

"It should be finished now." Holmes turned to his table of pipettes and glass tubes suspended from metal stands. The pale green contents bubbled in round-bottomed flasks above alcohol burners. Donning a glove, the sleuth lifted one blackened tube from its place above a flame. Taking a glass dish from a stack of many like it, he began to scrape the charcoal out.

"Add seventeen percent buffered saline solution," Holmes mumbled to himself as he poured liquid from a tall beaker into the dish. The detective stirred the mix with a glass rod. Then he took another syringe and sucked up some of the mud-colored liquid.

"Wait. Stop!" Peachy said. "You're not actually going to shoot that dotty goo into Danny's arm, are you?"

"Not before it's tested." With that, Holmes lifted a mouse from the box. "If this rodent can sustain the injection and lives for more than ten minutes, then I might have a viable antidote." Peachy took a seat on the sofa and turned away as Holmes jabbed the mouse with the needle. Holmes returned and sat in his rocking chair, a box containing the test animal on his lap. "Now we wait."

Holmes tried to start a conversation, but Peachy did not feel like talking. He stared at the mouse just as he and Duff had watched Danny all night. *Ten minutes can drag on an immensely long time,* Peachy thought.

Holmes rose at last, putting the box on the floor. He walked across the room, donned his hat, and dropped the test tube of blackened powder into his coat pocket. "Come, Carnehan," he said with quietly triumphant pride, "let's go save our friend."

Peachy jumped from his seat and bolted down the stairs. "Crikey, Mr. Holmes, I sure am glad you're on our side!"

"Funny. Everyone keeps telling me that." Outside, Holmes signaled for a cab. As Peachy was climbing up, the detective said, "I've forgotten the beaker of buffered solution. I'll be right down."

"Oh, let me," Peachy said, scrambling out of the hansom cab. "I can go quicker. What is it I'm fetching?"

"The tall glass cylinder with the measurements marked on the side. It's full of a special saltwater mixture."

Holmes laughed as Peachy dashed back inside and up the stairs. The boy swung around on the bannister as he swooped past the corner into the sitting room. He saw the beaker resting on an end table and grasped it, then glanced at the box on the floor. His breath froze in his lungs. "Holmes!" he screamed. "Holmes! Mr. Holmes!"

The test mouse lay on the bottom of the cage, still, unmoving, dead.

Holmes reentered the room, already suspecting what Peachy had found. "Blast! There's no time for this. I don't have time to make another."

"What then, Mr. Holmes? What do we do now?" Peachy was crying again, his voice choked up. "Danny is dying . . ."

Holmes yelped. "I don't know what to do! I've worked all night on this, and I don't know! Why don't you leave me alone? What am I missing? What?" The detective pulled straight up on a handful of his dark brown hair.

Peachy ran out of Baker Street with Holmes shouting after him, "Carnehan, I'm sorry! There must be another way. I'm sorry." But Peachy ran on.

With a snap of his fingers that indicated a sudden decision, the detective swept abruptly down the stairs.

Returning to the cab that still waited at the curb he said, "Take me to Seven Dials!"

———

Clair clutched at Danny's hand as he lay still in the hospital bed. He had been so restless all day and the night before that she worried that his calm now was a bad sign. *Dear God,* she prayed silently, *please help Danny.*

Duff had finally left the room when he became too hungry to stay. One of the nurses had heard his stomach growling, and he followed her when she mentioned food. Clair laid her pale cheek against Danny's hand. The heat from his fever radiated on her face as if she held a glowing coal just inches away. Alone with him now, she suddenly felt an urge to explain how she felt about him.

"Daniel Wiggins, you can't die. I don't know what we would do without you, especially me. I know I should tell you this when you're awake, but I've been afraid. You're very special to me, Danny. You and Peachy and Duff have been important to me since we first met. You saved my life then, and now you've done it again. But, oh, Danny, I can't thank you if you don't wake up. You'll make it, Daniel, you have to."

She rose and walked to the window. Danny rolled over and moaned. Allowing her hopes to pull her, she turned back, convinced that Danny would be awake. But Danny had merely taken another feverish turn, sweating and shivering at the same time. Clair exhaled slowly, tears glistening in her eyes as she dropped her gaze to the floor.

Duff returned through the curtain, still chewing a bite of the roast chicken that had been lunch. Dr. Benson followed Duff in, walking briskly with thermometer in hand to Danny's bedside. "Clair," Duff said, "you should eat. The food here is good food. And the nurses are nice nurses. And they said that Daniel Wiggins would do better after I had some food. Maybe you should eat too."

Benson glanced at Clair and nodded, indicating that Duff was right. His kind eyes also showed that he would take care of Danny while she was away.

"Will you show me where to go, Duff?" she asked.

Duff looked at the bed. "I can stay with Danny, because I already . . ."

"But I don't know where to go. And maybe you could have more food . . . for Danny's sake." Duff nodded as he led the way back out of the room. Dr. Benson smiled and put his stethoscope in his ears.

His smile faded when he heard Danny's weak heartbeat. "Godspeed Mr. Holmes. May the Lord guide your research."

———

Peachy rushed past the green-uniformed porter and up the steps of the British Museum. The porter shouted for him to stop running, but Peachy neither slowed nor turned until he ran headlong into Mr. Dreyer, the curator of antiquities.

"Certainly, Mr. Carnehan," Dreyer replied to Peachy's breathless question. "I can show you exactly where he is." Peachy had come to the great museum in hopes of finding Patrick Gannon with a cure in hand. "Professor Gannon came in a rush and told me he was going to do research in the medical library. It's in one of the bays near the rear of the building." As he spoke,

Dreyer was turning a large ring of skeleton keys, looking for the one to fit the side door to the Reading Room. "Ah, here it is." The man fumbled with the iron rods, dropping and retrieving them twice.

"Please, sir," Peachy said with irritation. "It's very important that we hurry."

"Of course. Your friend, is it? What a dreadful shame."

Peachy glared up at him. "Not yet it isn't. Please hurry."

"Of course."

They reached a small door that looked as though it might lead to a closet. "Now don't get lost in here." Peachy did not like his joke, but when the door was opened, Peachy realized it had not been said in jest.

The room was gigantic. Two floors of ten shelves each circled the room, while the center was filled with row upon row of stacks too high for the boy to see over.

Like an auditorium in which the leather-bound volumes were the spectators, Peachy felt that he was the one on exhibition in the center. A musty smell instantly filled his nose. In the dim lighting, the room seemed to have no end.

"Is this the way?" Peachy asked. Dreyer nodded, and Peachy headed down the center aisle. As he ran, he called for Gannon, hoping to save some time. There was no answer from Gannon.

Peachy could see various strange titles on the shelves as he ran past: *Principia Medicina; Ye Ancient and Accepted Sovereign Remedy for Black Water Fever; The Greek Specific against Scrofula, unabridged, untranslated; Preser-*

vation Techniques in the Valley of the Kings; Jaundice in Indonesia.

At the far end of the long row the shelving stopped, and an old, brown-painted, spiral staircase led to the second floor. Peachy was just about to run up when Gannon appeared at the top. The boy stopped on the bottom step, looking up at the archaeologist.

"Hello, Peachy," Gannon said. "I'm glad you've come. I believe I've found something that might work. It's in a copy of an old Egyptian text, and I've deciphered enough of the script to find that it talks of many poisonous snakes and their antivenoms. But my specialty is in ancient Persian artifacts, and it will take me a while longer to work out the rest."

"Do you need help carrying books?"

"No, thank you. I'll be right down." Gannon walked away from the stairs to a table that was just visible at the top. He picked up a dusty, pigskin-covered tome.

As Gannon reached the small desk, Peachy saw a strange brown whip lash at Gannon's leg from beneath the oak chair. Gannon cried out, and Peachy knew at once that the man had been bitten by a snake.

As Gannon clutched the wound on his leg, he was bitten again. Peachy watched in horror as Gannon's body spasmed, his back stiffening. He fell forward, slithering down the stairs in a snakelike slide and landed on his head. His body then came to a stop at Peachy's feet.

Peachy did not look to see if Gannon was still alive. The boy knew he would need help right away for the snakebites. Peachy bolted back down the long aisle to the small side door, yelling for the curator. "Mr. Dreyer," he screamed. "Fetch a doctor! Mr. Gannon's been bitten! Fetch a doctor! Mr. Dreyer!"

Dreyer opened the door just as Peachy reached it. "What is it now?"

"It's Mr. Gannon," Peachy panted. "A snake . . . he fell."

Dreyer pushed past Peachy and ran down the length of the shelving back to where Gannon lay unmoving. In one swift move, Dreyer heaved Gannon's body over his shoulder and carried him back to a bench by the door. "Stay with him, Carnehan. I'll need to fetch help." Dreyer laid Gannon down, and Peachy looked at the archaelogist's face. He was quite still, though his features were contorted with pain. Peachy shivered and turned away.

Somewhere among the heaps of cures and remedies, a small, poisonous reptile flowed unobserved.

A few minutes passed, and then the clanging of a bell announced the arrival of a horse-drawn ambulance. Two men in white jackets entered the library carrying a stretcher. They were followed by a red-faced doctor toting his black bag. The physician waved an ammonia bottle under Gannon's nose and pressed a small vial of liquid to the unresponsive lips. But it was already too late: Patrick Gannon was dead.

———

After Gannon's body had been removed by the ambulance, Dreyer sent word to the London Zoological Society to send their reptile keeper to capture the snake. Peachy sat in a chair near the door, listening to their distant, echoing talk.

122 • *Jake & Luke Thoene*

"I can't find a thnake anywhere," said Rajeev Goa, the reptile keeper. "Ith quite likely that it eth-caped through a hole in the wall or a drainage grate."

Dreyer nodded absentmindedly, obviously upset by Gannon's death. The curator returned to Peachy's side. "Would you like a cab to take you back to your home?"

Peachy shook his head in misery and despair. "Isn't there anyone who can decipher the book that Mister Gannon was reading?"

"No, son. I'm sorry, there just isn't. I'm sure there's been a full translation made at one point, but work like that comes and goes . . . no one cares about ancient remedies. London has the leading medical practices of the entire world, and there's nothing that could have been done two thousand years ago that can't be done today. If there's a cure for your friend, modern science will find it."

Peachy nodded and walked blindly through the door toward the main entrance of the museum. Dreyer followed, hailing a hansom cab for him and paying the driver in advance to take Peachy back to Waterloo Road Ragged School.

TEN

HOLMES ARRIVED again at Seven Dials. Just off the southward pointing spoke of the wheel, he hurried up to a small, black door and banged on the panel. There was no answer. The nearby windows were shuttered tight and covered with grates. Then Holmes spotted a hole in the rusted remains of an ivy-covered wrought iron fence to the right of the entrance. He wrestled his way through it.

Trudging knee high in snapping, dried-up leaves and sprigs of vine, the detective used a glove to brush cobwebs and coal soot away from a nearly opaque window. Inside an almost bare sitting room there were no signs that anyone had been there in years. He saw a generous accumulation of trash left behind by previous occupants. A warped, water-soaked ceiling hung precariously above the empty wooden floor. On the twisted floorboards were broken bits of furniture, torn scraps of faded curtains, and bits of plaster from walls that leaned inward.

Holmes made his way to another windowsill, desperate to find a way in. The panes of glass in the parlor window were too small to use unless he smashed them all, and the metal frame that surrounded them was too tough to break out. He'd have to find another way.

Beneath his feet in the weed-choked yard, an iron grate covering a drain creaked under his weight. These bars were the security for the basement windows. The private investigator kicked free the dead plants that covered the barrier and knelt to the ground. He pressed his face to the bars, peering into the blackness.

"There must be a way in," he muttered in frustration.

The rusty platform creaked and moaned from his twelve-stone mass. The crossbar that supported the grate was deeply cut into the weathered concrete. Holmes could see broken-off fragments that had crumbled to the ground beneath the grate. While he watched, additional chunks bounced from the hard bottom of the light well over to dusty panes of glass that Holmes had not even noticed.

He pulled on the barricade from the side, wiggling it loose. Holmes shook the panel, dropping more cubes of debris. It was still cemented in too tightly to pull up, so the detective tried a different approach. He held on to the spiked fence bars to support his weight and began to bounce.

The pounding of his boot heels forced the metal to bend at the corners. It creaked louder with every jump. Layers of dark red corroded metal flaked off. Then, all at once, the grate folded at the middle, broke loose from the sides, and fell heavily into the hole.

Holmes struggled to keep his grip. His hands slipped, and the rotten frame of the fence bowed, pulling the wrought iron across the hole. Propelled by the added weight of the fence, the grate crashed through the basement window.

Hanging upside-down above the uncovered light well, Holmes struggled to get free of the ivy and wire that entangled him. The drop was quite far, and he would risk breaking his neck if he landed badly. As he gingerly worked to free himself, Holmes found that he could not unhook his feet and hold on to the side of the well at the same time. This was not a neighborhood in which to call for help either. Just as the detective was planning his next move, the decision was made for him: The weeds that snared his legs tore free and he fell. Holmes landed heavily on his shoulders.

He lay motionless on the ground among the rubble. Holmes checked all his parts to determine that he was intact before he attempted to move. A bruised ankle, smashed against the concrete wall by his ungainly plunge, seemed to be the only injury. He rubbed the joint. Already it was swelling and soon would be too stiff to run on.

Sitting up and studying the broken window, Holmes was pleased. The grate had made a perfect shot that could not have been better if he had aimed. The master sleuth climbed through, scooting carefully on his rear. He dropped several more feet to the cellar floor, bouncing on his good foot when he landed.

Looking around the room was difficult in the darkness, and it was even harder to breathe in all the dust. By the looks of the shavings, the room had been used as a furniture mill. *It's a wonder how anyone worked in such conditions,* he mused.

Holmes hobbled over to a staircase, where a glimmer of light showed from above. Measuring his ankle against the flight of stairs, the detective ignored the pain and hurried to the top.

On the ground floor, in the same room that he had seen through the grimy window, Holmes examined the possibilities. He could go up further or back down to what looked like a set of offices at the ground level. He chose the offices.

Holmes drew his revolver and tiptoed into the hallway. In a small room on the right sat an empty desk that tilted on three crumbling legs. The disintegrating layers of the laminated wood top peeled back like the cover of a book that had been read dozens of times.

Trudging onward, Holmes searched for the man with the key to Danny's miracle. The investigator passed a couple more rooms like the first but came up empty-handed. The end of the hallway was stacked with crates of records and boxes of rotting trash, which filled the space from floor to ceiling. Holmes waded through it all to get to the very end but again found nothing.

Frustration and worry rose as Holmes knew that time was not on his side. He needed an answer, and quickly, if he were to save Danny's life. On his way out of the offices level, Holmes spotted a map hanging on the wall by the door. When he examined it closely, he saw that it was a floor plan of the offices, production rooms, and what looked to be a set of apartments. The flats of living space were shown on the plan to be in a separate building but attached at the third floor by a suspended hallway.

Stepping gingerly on his sore ankle, Holmes set out

for the apartments. Back to the staircase and up two flights, just as the plans had shown. There he found the hallway depicted on the map. It was long and narrow, with no windows or doors, except the one at the end.

Preparing himself for a confrontation, Holmes cocked his revolver and crept to the entry. Hearing a voice from the other side of the door, the sleuth knew he had found his man. He heard a man's voice with a distinctly Middle Eastern accent—it had to be his quarry.

Another man spoke. This one sounded younger. The investigator waited to see if there were any more opponents in the room.

When, after a minute, Holmes heard the older caution the younger to keep his voice down, he decided it was time to act. He kicked in the door, groaning with the pain from his bad leg.

The door swung wide, crashing into a chair. The eyes of the two occupants opened wide, resembling yellow marbles. The older man tried to kick the door shut again, slowing Holmes, while the other scurried out the open window to the fire escape. Holmes fired two shots that struck the window frame, discouraging the older man from also attempting to go through the opening.

Aiming a blow at the side of the detective's head, the Persian showed that he was unafraid of the revolver. Another shot, triggered in the struggle, blasted into the floor, and then another ripped a foot-long sliver into the ceiling. Holmes's quarry pounced on top of him, wrestling for control of the gun. The investigator's finger slipped on the guard, firing yet another shot into the door.

Holmes rolled on his back, bashing the man in the

face with the gun. But the blow loosened his grip, and the Webley went flying across the floor, sliding to a stop just below the window.

The man dove for the gun, but Holmes grabbed his legs. Holmes scrambled over the man in a life-or-death race for the revolver. The Persian threw back his head, butting Holmes in the jaw. The detective's teeth cracked together, and he tasted blood. His vision went momentarily black.

When Holmes opened his eyes again, the Persian was standing over him with the gun. Exhausted and knowing the power of his pistol at such close range, Holmes dared not move. "I know you, Zagros," he said, "leader of the Guardians."

The dark-haired man with the scraggly beard moved around Holmes so that his back was toward the window. He waved the revolver in the detective's face.

"It doesn't matter about me," Holmes said with resignation, "but a boy's life is at stake. He's been bitten by a snake and will die if I don't get him the antidote."

"The Guardian is angry because the crown has not been returned," the frenzied Persian yelled as sweat poured from his face. He held the gun tightly and jabbed at Holmes with the muzzle. "The dying will not stop until the crown has been returned!"

"That may be," Holmes said coolly, "but the boy. He had nothing to do with the loss of the crown. Why should he pay for what others do wrong?"

"If you know me as you say, you know that we do not make war on children, nor want anything except the return of what belongs to our people. It is the curse at work from whence come the snakes. But tell me truly: If I tell you what you wish to know, can you arrange the release of my comrade from the depths of Old Bailey? We did not cause any death, and he has done no harm."

"Yes," Holmes agreed. "But if you have lied to me, I will hunt you down again."

The dark-skinned man reflected on this exchange. There was a long pause, and then he nodded slowly. "You are a man of honor. All right then. The only cure for the boy is in the blood of another man who has been bitten and survived."

Elam Zagros threw the gun to the floor, then turned and dove out the window.

Sherlock Holmes picked himself up slowly and placed the revolver back in his pocket. "Danny must have blood from someone who's been bitten by the snake and lived," he said aloud. "How on earth will I find a man like that in the heart of London?"

As he staggered out of the building, Holmes reflected on Danny's condition. As strong as the boy was, he could only survive another few hours, and it seemed there was little hope left for him.

Holmes limped down to the corner to catch a taxi. He remembered how he had yelled at Peachy just when the boy needed him the most. Sadly conscious of his failure, the detective set out to find Peachy and to communicate the defeat of his search. Together they would go to be with Danny at the end.

———

When Peachy arrived back at the school, he was in a dismal mood. He wanted to be alone but somehow needed to be with someone else. He considered going back to the hospital but could not bear to see Danny in so much pain and so obviously nearing the end of the road.

Peachy walked through the large front doors, heading directly up the stairs to the sleeping quarters. Upon reaching the top floor, he was greeted by several classmates who usually would not notice his arrival. Of course they had all heard of Danny's accident. In a detached way, Peachy thought how tragedy and sorrow sometimes caused people to reach out and comfort others. News spread quickly among those who sold the papers, and over half of the boys who lived at the school held jobs related to the London dailies.

One boy, Geoffrey Morris, spoke kindly to him. "Hello, Peachy. How are you?"

"Fine," Peachy lied. He walked to his bed as quickly as he could. All eyes in the room watched him. Geoffrey followed him.

"Peachy, I heard about Danny. I'm real sorry." Not knowing how else to help, he offered Peachy a piece of the apple that he was holding. "It's good," he said. "Take it."

"Morris, why don't you go away?" Peachy snapped. "I'm not hungry." There was nothing his classmates could do to help; nothing anyone could do.

That fact angered Peachy. Usually he was able to help himself and his friends out of tight situations by his cunning or sharp wit. Now he realized that neither of those traits would help Danny recover. Danny was left to the skill of others and the mercy of God. *But there must be something we overlooked,* he thought, *something we're forgetting.*

Headmaster Ingram entered the room. Peachy

rolled over on his cot and covered his head with pillow. The schoolmaster approached anyway. "Peachy? Do you want to talk about it?"

Peachy did not remove the pillow. He wanted to talk all right, but he did not want to cry. The tears were nearly brimming over his eyelids as it was. "Please, go away. Talking doesn't help. Nothing helps."

"I know," Ingram said softly. "Please, Peachy, remember that God cares about Danny, just as he cares about you. Dinner begins soon. You need to eat so that you can think clearly. You'll feel better if you join us all downstairs."

"Sure," Peachy lied. Secretly, he was glad that everyone would be leaving the room. When he heard the last descending footstep, he began to cry. *Why? Why? Why?* he repeated in his mind. What would he do without Danny around? Danny was like his brother, as well as his best friend.

The cot creaked as someone sat down next to Peachy. He felt a large, comforting hand on his back. "Carnehan," Holmes's voice was soft, "I'm sorry." Peachy's heart began to pound and he sobbed. Holmes had probably just come from the hospital to tell him it was over. Holmes held the boy's shoulder in his long fingers. "I know," he said, "I know. If only there were a way to find someone . . ." His voice trailed off.

Peachy sniffed and uncovered his head. "He's not gone?"

"No, not yet . . ." Holmes caught himself. "No," he said more firmly.

The two sat in silence for a time. It seemed so unfair to Peachy that Danny should be dying. After all, the snake keeper, Goa, had survived many attacks. Peach wondered, *How could that be?* "Just luck?" he mused aloud.

"Hmmm?"

Peachy wiped his eyes. "Nothing. Just thinking about the snake keeper we met."

Holmes felt a tinge of hope flicker in his chest. "What about him, Carnehan?"

"He told us that only one in a hundred people survive bites from the hearth viper."

"And is he that one?" Holmes asked, standing up and rocking the cot. "Did this snake keeper survive a bite from a hearth viper?"

Peachy detected his excitement. "So he said. Why? Is it important?"

"Dear boy!" the sleuth exclaimed. "It means there's someone in London who can save your friend!"

"What? I don't unders . . ."

Holmes jerked him up by his arm. "No time to waste! Come with me and I'll explain on the way. In our haste lies Danny's second chance at life!"

ELEVEN

RAJEEV GOA'S DAY had been long. It had started at six in the morning when he cleaned the snake, lizard, and turtle cages, one by one. Now it was seven in the evening, and he planned to take his wife to the British Museum that night to see the Jewelled Peacock of Persia in one of the only public shows to be held in London. Goa removed the apron and leather gloves he was wearing and began to wash up at a sink in the work area behind the cases.

So many supplies to put away, he thought, *so much work to do.* He had to feed the reptiles before he went home, but he decided to put everything away before he did so. Then he could leave immediately after he finished.

He walked to his locker and removed his boots, taking out a pair of black leather dress shoes. He folded his apron neatly and placed it in the locker, closing the door. He moved slowly back to the "feed box," as they called it.

In it were hundreds of live mice, which he knew to be the only thing his snakes would eat.

"Feeding row-th three, five, and th-even," he said to himself, calculating the necessary number of mice. Goa picked up an aluminum pail with a wire mesh cover from a stack by the feed box and dipped it in. He scooped up a bucketful of scampering rodents. "Th-orry," he said to each of the mice as he walked along the rows, opening the doors and placing one inside each cage.

Goa always finished this task feeling a bit disheartened. He loved the snakes but wished they could learn to eat vegetables. He sighed at the unlikely thought and reminded himself for the thousandth time that it was a wasted wish.

Goa's flat lay across Regents Park to the south. He never took a cab but rather enjoyed the walk every evening after he finished work. The reptiles' caretaker was sixty years old now, and the walk seemed to grow longer by the month. He liked the stroll though, since it gave him time to think after being so busy all day. Tonight he would contemplate the repeated trips he had made to the British Museum recently to capture the dangerous snakes that kept appearing there. Goa was especially saddened when he remembered the news about the boy bitten by the viper.

As Goa passed through the turnstile at the exit, he waved to the security guard on duty there. Breathing the fresh night air brought hunger pains to his stomach. He wondered what his wife, Felicia, had prepared for supper.

Felicia Anne Goa had been his wife for thirteen years. They had first met when she was his nurse after a particularly bad bite he had sustained removing a hooded cobra from the Queen's Gardens at Buckingham. Felicia told him when he finally opened his eyes after three weeks that she had not left his bedside while he battled for life.

His doctors had originally thought that the poison had destroyed Goa's power of speech. He communicated by pad and pencil with Felicia, and they fell in love. The truth was that he had refused to speak, fearing that his beautiful nurse would laugh him away the first time he came to an "s" word. When he finally realized he would go crazy if he did not speak again, he wrote in great fear and confusion, "I can talk, but it's not a pretty sight."

Felicia had responded by whispering in his ear, "Darling, have you looked in a mirror recently? Two months in bed with no barber? Had I wanted a pretty sight, I'd have gone away long ago." The medical staff joked that Rajeev had prolonged his recovery purposely so he could stay with Felicia as long as possible.

"I am a lucky man," Rajeev said aloud to the summer night. He was nearing the middle of the park, and here in the open grassy area he could see that the sky was full of stars. As he gazed upward he said, "Thank you, God. I petition you again for a chance to repay you."

Then Goa heard a strange noise behind him. It sounded like thunder rolling across the grass, coming closer and closer to him. He stopped and turned around slowly, afraid of what he might see.

His face went white when he saw a horse and rider charging at him. The mounted man was plainly going to spur right over top of him. *Thieves,* he thought. *How strange that I will die this way.* Knowing that to run would cause him to be trampled from behind, Goa preferred to face the onslaught.

He was startled when the rider abruptly drew rein, slid the horse to an awkward halt, and called his name, "Mr. Goa!"

———

When Peachy dismounted from the horse, he explained to a very shaken Rajeev Goa that there was no time to lose, that Danny's life depended on haste. Peachy helped the snake keeper onto the horse, then pulled himself up behind.

"Wherever did you get thith animal?" Goa asked as they trotted uncomfortably back across the sod.

"I took him from the cabbie that brought us to the zoo."

"U-th? Who i-th 'u-th'?"

"None other than Mr. Sherlock Holmes himself," Peachy said. Then he kicked with both legs to force the animal into a faster canter.

When they reached the entrance to the zoo, Goa saw the hansom cab, detached from the horse, that lay at a strange angle with its hitch resting on the cobblestones. Holmes looked impressed at Peachy's performance, but the cabbie was less than amused. They reharnessed the horse and clattered down the street in the direction of Saint Bartholomew's Hospital.

———

Rajeev Goa's arm ached. Dr. Benson had withdrawn several large syringes of his blood for injection into Danny. The crimson fluid was separated into its component parts and mixed with Holmes's now perfected antivenom serum. It seemed to require an enormous amount of blood to produce one small test tube of serum, but Goa was happy to help in any way he could.

The snake handler tried not to show that he doubted anything would come of the experimental cure. "What kind of remedy would thi-th be, Mr. Holme-th?"

"I learned it from a Persian man, Mr. Goa. And I thank you again for contributing." Though Holmes was also uncertain if it would work, he did not express his fears to the children.

Clair had been so relieved to see something being done for Danny that now she slept in a chair by the door. Duff was downstairs in the cafeteria eating again, having taken Dr. Benson's earlier advice to heart. Peachy was the only one in the room paying close attention to Danny, as though he would see him get better right before his eyes.

Holmes knew there would be a critical period in which the antidote would either work or else his worst fears would come true. With this in mind, he spoke. "Miss Avery . . . Clair?" She opened her eyes. "Do you have transportation arranged?"

"Yes, Mr. Holmes, an officer has been waiting for me downstairs by order of my father."

"Very well then, I suggest you go home now. We've done all we can do here. I'm quite sure we will be able to visit Wiggins tomorrow."

"That's a great idea, Mr. Holmes," Peachy said, yawning. "I could use a rest."

"Not a chance, Carnehan! We still have work to do," Holmes replied. Peachy rolled his eyes. "We must stop this incident from repeating itself. We are off to the British Museum!" Holmes turned away from the red-haired boy. "Miss Avery, do you think you might drive Mr. Goa back to his home in your carriage?" She nodded. "Good. Then we shall be off. Dr. Benson, I shall arrive at first light tomorrow." The great detective added a whispered word in the doctor's ear and received a frowning nod in reply. "Then good night to you," Holmes concluded, and he swept the Baker Street Irregulars out of the room.

———

"Move that one over there," Curator Dreyer ordered. Security personnel were placing the snake-proof fencing around the area where people would be viewing the Peacock Crown. "Make sure the sections are good and tight."

No one in an official position would admit to belief in the curse, and yet . . . the crown had not been returned to Persia, so precautionary measures were in order. A few brawny workers muscled the fencing into the locations that Dreyer indicated.

It was speculated to be the largest public gathering ever for a display of its kind. By the looks of the crowd waiting outside, the numbers were already four times the size of any prior exhibitions despite the fact that adults were being charged a crown each for admission—about a day's wages—and children half a crown. In light of the masses of people, Curator Dreyer had cleared the enormous floor of the copper-domed Reading Room for the nighttime display of the crown.

"Tightly!" Dreyer shouted again, unnecessarily.

"Careful with those shelves and tables," he also commanded. "Take them to the storeroom."

One of the more fearful workers disagreed. "Not a chance am I going back down there! It's a right proper breedin' ground for snakes!"

"You don't have a choice in the matter," Dreyer announced harshly, "unless you wish to be dismissed!" Everyone noticed that the curator made no move toward the basement himself, but no one commented on this fact.

"A bloke died in here when it was light," another worker complained. "What chance have we got against blooming snakes and the ruddy curse in the blinking dark?"

"I assure you," Dreyer insisted, "we have thoroughly searched the premises. There are no more snakes, *and there is no curse!*" The curator fairly screamed the last half of his sentence, but somehow it was not believable in light of the snake-proof fencing. Even Dreyer seemed to catch the irony. "Oh, very well then, move the tables back by the offices. You there," he called to the dismissed worker, "don't leave. Just take the furniture into the back hallway."

Minutes later the floor was entirely clear of shelves, sofas, and reading tables. Dreyer ordered that the other Persian pieces be brought out and set up on their displays. Specially hired handlers gently wheeled out an eight-and-a-half-foot tall clay urn, which dated from the Persian empire of Ardashir I. It was placed carefully behind the safety barricades. Other objects, including a collection of bronze spearheads and twisted copper bracelets, were added to the array.

The room was filled with one-thousand-year-old artifacts, but greatest of all, the highlight of the entire exhibition, was the Jewelled Peacock of Persia. The crown was placed in the center of the Reading Room on a high pedestal and was the focus of the entire room. Six uniformed guards were stationed by the security barricades which surrounded it.

Dreyer took a deep breath, then opened the doors to let the crowd in. People flocked in by the hundreds. Each one gladly dropped his or her crowns and shillings in the box to see what the newspapers sensationally called "the most horribly evil artifact in the history of the world." Dreyer stood back and watched, while talking to Macintire.

"Why anyone would want to risk his or her life to come see such a malicious piece of metal is beyond me," Dreyer remarked.

"It's the excitement," Macintire argued, "the danger. People say they don't believe in curses, yet they are curious to see something so powerful that it can take a human life. And it's not just the people with ordinary lives who want excitement. The rich, even those who could afford to go Persia themselves, are here too. It's about money in exchange for thrills. It's a business," he concluded, smiling proudly.

The money tills were filling so quickly that they had to be carried away and emptied constantly. "As bad as this curse affair has been, it's good business for everyone, including you and the museum," Macintire added. "Don't forget that your precious institution gets half of the take."

Curator Dreyer shook his head with disbelief at

Macintire's callous attitude. "The way things are going, there'll be a lot fewer of us to see the end result. But perhaps when no new sensation or disaster occurs today, things will calm down a bit."

Macintire cocked his head in consideration but said nothing. His eyes suddenly narrowed, and he said, "If you'll excuse me a moment. . . . I'll be right back."

———

The clattering hooves of the carriage horse almost drowned out the conversation between Holmes and Peachy in the back of the hansom cab on the way to the British Museum.

Holmes nudged the boy's arm. "Here, take these." The detective extended two heavy, round sticks about eight inches long, coated in dark red wax.

"What are they?" Peachy asked, feeling the blunt end where an obvious fuse stuck out. "Explosives?"

"No," Holmes corrected, "flares. Miners' torches, actually. They'll keep the snakes away, if there are any."

"So you think something else will happen?"

"There are still at least two Persians on the loose," Holmes replied. "And I believe they will stop at nothing to recover the crown. And that may not be all . . ."

Two deaths already, and Danny barely clinging to life! It made Peachy angry that people spoke of the jewelled crown with excitement. As far as he was concerned, the wicked object should be sent back to Persia or thrown into the ocean. Even worse was the way the newspapers publicized the misfortune. Why, they followed the sinister events almost like a cricket match, keeping score: the

Guardians of the Peacock, three; the British, zero. He felt sick and infuriated at the same time.

"Security will be so tight tonight," Peachy remarked, changing the subject to keep his thoughts from Danny. "How would anyone ever be able to steal the crown and get away?"

"They might find a way," Holmes answered thoughtfully. "I just hope we're not too late."

The carriage rolled up the circular driveway at the museum. Even from a distance Holmes and Peachy could tell something had already gone terribly wrong. The lights were out in the building while people ran screaming from the entrance, spooking the horses.

Holmes rapped on the roof of the cab. "Stop here!" Flinging a handful of coins at the driver, Holmes and Peachy leaped out.

Guards and security personnel fought to hold the barricades that protected the ancient pieces of art and history from being trampled. Holmes and Peachy spotted Dreyer standing on a table by a pillar and hurried to him.

"Dreyer," Holmes yelled, "what's happened here?"

Dreyer looked relieved to see Holmes. "The lights," he panted. "They went off, someone shouted about snakes, and the whole place erupted at once."

"Are there any snakes?" Peachy yelled over the screams of the crowd.

"Yes, I mean, I don't know," Dreyer said, frantically scanning the floor from the safety of the tabletop. "I haven't seen any yet, but when everyone started to yell . . ."

Holmes cut him off. "Where's Lestrade?"

"In the panic someone jumped the barricade and

stole the crown. The inspector went chasing after him, up to the second floor."

"Carnehan, keep a sharp lookout!" Holmes instructed. "Don't be afraid to light one of those torches while I go to see what I can do."

"Where's Macintire?" Peachy asked Dreyer.

"I don't know." The curator shook his head. "He left just before all of this pandemonium happened, and I haven't seen him since. I do hope he hasn't fallen victim to the curse."

Peachy considered the possibilities that maybe Macintire was trapped or injured or . . . "Any idea where he went?" he asked, pulling the flares from his pocket.

"In his office possibly. I don't know."

Peachy lit the first torch. It popped, then fizzled and cracked until it burned a bright red flame. "I'm going to find him."

"No, wait," Dreyer called. "Do be careful!" The terrified man made no move to stop Peachy or to get down from his perch.

Maroon-colored smoke poured from the torch and rose to the ceiling as Peachy navigated his way through the mess and clutter that now obstructed the floor. A thousand bleak images filled his mind: snakes crawling over one another, jumping out at him from the dark. He saw their fangs dripping with venom . . . perhaps they were behind him now. Trying to walk and watch over both shoulders at the same time, he ran headfirst into an Etruscan statue, giving himself a black eye. After that accident, Peachy paid more attention to his path.

Remembering where Macintire's office was located, the boy made his way slowly, carefully searching the floor as he walked. He reached the hallway and turned right. The corridor was piled high with tables and shelves that had been removed from the library for the exhibition. Peachy made sure there were no snakes hiding underneath them before he stepped around them.

He walked to Macintire's office and turned the knob. The door resisted at first, then swung inward with a noisy groan. There, hunched over his desk in the red glow of the torchlight, was Douglas Macintire.

Something was wrong in the position of the man and in the unnatural silence. "Mr. Macintire?" Peachy called, but the man did not move.

A loud bang echoed through the quiet hall, and the museum lights flicked on again. The sudden noise had spun Peachy toward the stairs, but he turned around again slowly to face the office. There on the desk, Douglas Macintire lay facedown over a crushed basket. The desktop, the promoter's head, and his shoulders were covered with dozens of small, brown, hissing hearth vipers.

Peachy let out a scream at the gruesome sight. Though he instantly slammed the door shut, the scene was frozen in his mind. The jaws of several snakes were still latched onto Macintire's body, still pumping venom into a cause that had long since been accomplished.

Peachy dropped the burning torch, hoping it would keep any snakes from slithering out under the door. Then he ran to find Holmes. In a flash all the mystery became clear: the basket . . . the crowd that grew with each ac-

cident . . . the mysterious reappearances of the snakes
. . . even Gannon's untimely death. It all made sense
now. Peachy sprinted even faster to locate Sherlock
Holmes.

EPILOGUE

PEACHY JUMPED AWAY from the bed, frightened by the sudden way Danny's eyes flicked open. It was the morning after Macintire's death.

"Blimey, where am I?" Danny wondered aloud.

"You're in the hospital, mate. You've been dead asleep for days."

"I'm starving."

Duff awoke from where he slept on the floor at Danny's bedside. When his tousled head popped up, it gave Peachy another scare.

"Crikey, Duff," Peachy said, "why didn't you go home last night?"

"No one took me," replied Duff. "I'm not . . . it's not . . . I can't walk myself. It's scary at night. Danny slept here too." Peachy laughed.

Sherlock Holmes walked into the room carrying flowers. He was followed by Dr. Benson in a fresh white lab coat. "Ah, Wiggins," Holmes said, "finally you're awake! You've been so sleepy the past few days. We could have used your help." Danny managed a tired grin. "How do you feel?"

"I'm hungry," Danny repeated.

"Good," Peachy said. "He's said that twice now. He's telling the truth."

Benson came toward Danny with a thermometer, placing it in his mouth.

"What kind of food is this?" Danny joked.

"It's good to know you haven't lost your wit."

Danny looked around for the source of the feminine voice that had just insulted him. "Clair!" he mumbled over the thermometer as he tried to sit up in bed. "Are you hurt?"

"Why?" Clair joked again. "Are you making sure you weren't bitten for nothing?" Danny smiled and everyone in the room chuckled.

"I had a dream," Danny said. "I was running away from giant animals. The colors were spinning all around, and I couldn't run fast enough. One of them grabbed me . . . then all at once it stopped."

Peachy seemed to understand. "It must have been the antidote working."

"And I heard Clair's voice," Danny continued. Clair blushed. "I couldn't hear the words she spoke, but they seemed to drive the animals away for a short time."

Clair was relieved that Danny did not know what she had said. "Oh, Daniel. How silly."

Duff could not wait any longer to speak. "Danny, I asked God for you back. And he did it."

Danny smiled. "Yes, he did, Duff. Thank you."

"Danny, I think there's someone you ought to meet again," Holmes said as he walked out of the curtained partition. Danny waited quietly as he heard the door open. A moment later Holmes reappeared with Rajeev Goa behind him. "Daniel Wiggins. Meet your savior, Mr. Rajeev Goa."

Danny understood that somehow this battered old man had saved his life.

"Oh, no, by Jove. It was the Lord Je-thu-th," Goa protested.

"It was Mr. Goa's blood," Peachy explained, "that saved you from the snake. Blood to defeat poison, just like Headmaster Ingram said."

"Thank you," Danny said. "I can't thank you enough." Goa smiled at him, just nodding his head. "But now tell me about the case. Have you caught the Persians, Mr. Holmes? Did you capture all the snakes? Were there any more . . ."

"Slow down, Wiggins," Holmes cautioned. "You're liable to exhaust yourself. We can come back tomorrow to tell you how everything turned out." The detective turned from the bed. Danny caught his arm and spun him back around.

"No, sir. I want to know now!" Dr. Benson left the room to bring some food for Danny.

Everyone laughed. Peachy said, "What is there to tell? There is no curse. And the Persians were not responsible for any of the accidents."

Danny looked puzzled. "Who was then?"

Peachy glanced at Holmes, who nodded, then Peachy asserted, "None other than Douglas Macintire."

Danny's jaw dropped wide open. "Macintire was causing all of this? But why?"

"Publicity," Holmes continued. "The more scare

generated by the so-called curse, the more people wanted to see the crown. Publicity not only produced more money here but also set the stage for a world tour. He began with a simple magnetic device to raise the tail feathers and a single harmless snake."

"Does that mean Gannon was in on it too?" Danny asked.

"Yes," Peachy blurted. "But, Danny, Gannon was also bitten. He was not as lucky as you."

Holmes took up the explanation again. "You see, upon further interviews with Curator Dreyer, I came to realize that Gannon had to be in league with Macintire. They apparently had a falling out over how extreme the snake episodes became. For Gannon, the line was crossed when the elderly gentleman died . . . then when you were bitten as well . . ."

"What happened then?" Danny asked.

"Macintire overheard a conversation between Gannon and Dreyer in which Gannon was requesting more security. Macintire assumed that Gannon was selling him out or about to break down and give away the plot. At the first opportune moment, Macintire placed another snake where Gannon would be bitten by it."

"He was," Peachy continued, "but the venom took effect on him much faster than you, Danny. He died right away."

"True enough," Holmes said. "But it wasn't the bite that killed him. It was a broken neck. You see, when Gannon was bitten, he fell down the stairs in the medical library of the museum, landing directly on his head."

"So Gannon was working with Macintire," Danny mused. "That would explain why Gannon was in the basement. He must have put that snake in the lift. Well, where is Macintire now? In Old Bailey?"

Holmes shook his head. "During the confusion last night, the crown was stolen by a Persian who escaped in the panic. But that alarm was not of Macintire's doing. He was preparing another episode of the curse when the Guardians beat him to it and switched off the lights." Holmes paused. "From here, I think Carnehan could tell the story better."

Peachy looked proud. "I went looking for Macintire. I found him in his office, dead, bitten by more of the very snakes that had caused so much trouble before."

"I don't understand," Danny said. "Does that mean he was killed by someone else?"

"No," Peachy explained. "It was the way Macintire died that made me realize the truth. In the unexpected darkness he fell on a basket of snakes. In fact, some of them were still trapped inside."

Holmes summed it up. "We located a pair of leather handler's gloves under a hidden panel built into his office floor. That was where the snakes were kept."

"But please, where would Macintire have gotten all the th-nakes?" Rajeev Goa asked.

"Knowing that Macintire was American, a quick cable to the United States furnished the explanation," Holmes said. "It seems that Macintire was formerly known as Trenton Jacobs, a circus promoter in America. A publicity stunt seven years ago involving dangerous snakes left two patrons dead. He continued to raise venomous snakes in secret, changed his name, brought his schemes to England, and for a time was quite successful.

152 • Jake & Luke Thoene

But his greed got the better of him finally, and the crown was to be his greatest moneymaker yet."

Everyone was contemplating all the facts when Duff spoke. "I like circuses."

"So what has become of the crown?" Danny asked.

Holmes said, "I don't know where the crown is. But I know where it belongs, and I'll leave the pursuit . . . in Lestrade's capable hands."

Just then Dr. Benson returned with a trayful of food. "Everyone out now," he ordered. "This patient must eat and rest."

"Oh, Mr. Holmes," Danny hurriedly added, "one more thing."

"Yes?"

"What about the tunnel we found under the Lamb and Flag?"

"Oh yes, Mr. Holmes," Peachy agreed. "What did that have to do with the crown?"

"Not a thing. Your original theory was correct, Carnehan. Those men were after the jewelry store. Lestrade and his men pulled the shoring down and collapsed the tunnel, then sealed up the wall of the basement. So, congratulations. You foiled another crime by accident and probably saved my life in doing so. Good day, Wiggins, and get well quickly. I'm sure there will be more work to do soon."

GLOSSARY

B blimey—an expression of surprise
blinking—an expression to denote a negative
  attitude
bloke—a man
blooming—stupid, disgusting, impolite descriptive
  word
bobby—policeman
burk—to strangle
buzzer—a pickpocket or common thief
C chap—man
chavvy—street brat
cheerio—a friendly greeting
cor—an expression of surprise
crikey—an expression of surprise
cripes—an expression of surprise or disbelief
crusher—a guard
cut along—to hurry off, to get moving
D daft—crazy
dotty—crazy

dustup—row, fight

E eh, what—an expression that signals or asks for approval

G give over—quit, give up

glocky—crazy or unreliable

gob—mouth

granny—to know or guess

gull—to fool someone

H hanson cab—two-wheeled carriage pulled by one horse

having you on—kidding or fooling

K knap—steal

L leave off—stop or quit

lift—elevator

M mate—friend or pal

muck snipe—homeless beggar

N newsie—a paperboy

nipper—a young person, a child

nose—an informant

O oy—a word to get attention, like "Hey!"

P pish-tosh—an expression of disagreement, a comment that something is foolish

Q queue—a line of people

R rampsman—a mugger

right-o—an expression of agreement

rookery—a bad neighborhood, full of crime

rotter—a dishonest person, someone not to be trusted

ruddy—an expression to denote a negative attitude

S shindy—a fight

snaffle—to steal

starky—crazy

stone—weight equal to fourteen pounds
T tick—a moment, a second
  too right—an expression of agreement
  translator—a dealer in stolen goods
W what's on—an expression that means "What's up?"

Historical Notes

1) The British Museum—Founded in the year 1700, the British Museum houses the greatest collection of ancient artifacts in the world. From heroic-sized statues of biblical kings to classical Greek sculpture to the famous mummies, the museum is fabulously wealthy in antiquities. Many of its treasures were gathered under suspicious circumstances, and stories of evil curses attach to several of the objects stored there.

2) English Money—In the 1880s there were fifteen different coins in use. The basic units were the *penny* or *pence*, twelve of which made a *shilling*. Twenty shillings made a *pound*. (The pound coin was called a *sovereign*.) Other common coins were the *half crown*, equal to thirty pence or two and a half shillings, and the *crown*, equal to sixty pence or five shillings. Living in London cost a frugal person ten to twenty shillings per day.